THE COAST OF FEAR

Winter makes the rugged northeastern coast of Spain a desolate place—refuge for the escapees, the lost, the lonely . . . and for those who would seek them out.

Why would anyone be following me? Mio wondered as she drove along the dark coastal road, aware of the headlights behind her. And then a man darted into the glare waving wildly and shouting. She swerved, missed him, and heard the other car rush by. It would have driven her off the cliff . . .

Later Mio found herself seated at a table with four attractive men in a small hotel a short distance away from the "accident." Still shaken, she wondered if it was her imagination that the five of them—all strangers—had something in common.

Señor Ibáñez of the Guardia Civil was also observing these five. And his interest caused one of the five to flee, the others to join forces only to disband when death and holocaust came to the already wild and unpredictable Catalonian coast.

Scene: Spain

This novel has not appeared in any form prior to book publication.

K. G. Ballard

THE COAST
OF FEAR

Doubleday & Company, Inc.
Garden City, New York

This book is fiction,
and all the characters and incidents in it are entirely imaginary.

To KIT MULLER

With love, and with thanks
for her gracious generosity

"Some people are born to be hunters; there are others whose destiny is decided before their stars have merged, and it is preordained that they shall flee."

—Westerland

THE COAST OF FEAR

I

On the northeastern coast of Spain, above Barcelona and just south of France, is a stretch of rocky, cove-pierced coast known as the Costa Brava. Its length is variably described, but, strictly speaking, it runs some forty miles, from Blanes to Palafrugell. From the middle of May until the end of October this strip of coast line enjoys a tourist season rivaling that of the Riviera, and it is an inexpensive Riviera. During this almost six-month period it is possible—it is easy—to forget how bad is the single road, a rutted, rock-strewn, muddy path that traces the Mediterranean's profile but triples the distance by vaulting up and down like a roller-coaster track designed by a madman. The hostelries along the coast are pleasant, and at five dollars a day (three meals, tips, and taxes included) it is easy to dismiss their peculiarities; if the beautifully tiled bathroom runs out of water, one always has the so-blue Mediterranean to bathe in, and dinner at ten-thirty at night can be made to seem delightfully cosmopolitan once one's stomach has been bullied into acceptance. And at S'Agaró, about midway along the route, there is a truly luxury hotel, beautifully furnished, well run, and lovely to look at. Even this magnificent palace has its peculiarly Spanish idiosyncrasies, but for the too civilized it offers enough compensations to outweigh little inconveniences like doors that don't lock and generators that have temperament. For, as is true along the whole Catalonian coast, the scenery is wildly beautiful, the serving class (possibly the only Spaniards one will meet) are an entirely pleasant, non-*mañana* people, and the French, English, and Americans, the heaviest concentration usually being English, are surrounded by their own. (Despite tourists' oft-repeated assertion to the contrary they usually find it pleasant indeed to have their foreign flavors liberally diluted.)

. . . But in the winter, from November to April, the Costa Brava is a succession of small ghost towns, some with only a few hundred population, and that including the skeleton staffs of the hotels. The summer-chastened, Bianca-like Mediterranean becomes a winter virago that lashes shrewishly out at the bare cliffs and engulfs the small, vacuous beaches. And the rocky coast line—"*costa brava*" translates freely to "uncivilized coast"—that seems so pleasantly rugged in the summer reveals itself as being not very different from the rest of the northern half of Spain—barren and desolate . . . refuge, perhaps, for the escapees, the lost, the alone. And, perhaps, for those who would seek them out.

There was a peculiar crunching sensation . . . Mio felt the rock crumbling beneath her, heard the voracious sea beating against the cliff's edge, and then she wrenched the steering wheel violently to the left. The little car scrambled frantically back onto the road—the road Mio had thought

14

she saw in the darkness ahead but that had actually made a boomerang-angled left turn. There had been, she realized, *nothing* ahead—no reflector, not even a sea wall. Just space, and, beneath the space, rocks, and beneath the rocks, the Mediterranean.

She slowed the car to a crawl, and came to the conscious realization that she was afraid. As always with her, fear bred anger, this time at herself. The desk clerk at the hotel in Barcelona had warned her against this road. For that matter, in such vicious weather any road was foolishness unless the trip was imperative. Which made it, in her case, simple idiocy. That morning she had experienced one of her recurrent desires to start living, to stop stagnating. Since it was probably no more resolute a decision than usual, rushing off in all directions could certainly have waited for less inclement weather.

She set her jaw and peered through the yellow lace her headlights made of the night. The spot where she had so nearly gone over had been the ungraded, unbanked summit of that particular hazard. She was now coming to the hill's base—the breathing space, she thought wearily, before the next wild leap into mid-air. She was tired of scaling hills; she was tired of the lonely road, of the driving rain, of the horizontal wind off the too close sea. And—as she slowly took the precipitous right-hand turn onto the flat, she lifted her eyes to her rear-vision mirror—she was tired of the twin lights on the road behind her. He had just rounded the upper bend.

Her own turn removed the reflected glare from her eyes, but his presence was inescapably there. Still, the admission that there were lights persistently behind her made matters momentarily more bearable; she could examine the foolishness of the hitherto unacknowledged fear. Since there was only one road, why shouldn't there be lights? But why should anyone travel it? Well, she was traveling it, wasn't she? Yes, but she was being idiotic. Well, perhaps there was another idiot abroad. But why did the other idiot vary his speed to coincide with hers? For one dizzying kilometer she had driven at a speed suitable only to a California throughway on a June day; then she had slowed to about fifteen miles an hour. And the car behind had first matched her suicidal speed, and had then dropped with her into exaggerated caution.

Well—she shook her head in the darkness—the exterior difficulties were bad enough; she wouldn't permit herself to be further hampered by interior imaginings. No one could be following her, except accidentally. Incidentally. No one had any reason to follow her with intent. She would forget him, at least during those moments when he wasn't beamed in on her eyeballs. Concentrate on the road.

The road seemed momentarily sensible, except for potholes. Here on the flat where such a precaution was less necessary there was even a retaining wall on her right. Ahead, as far as she could see, all was level and straight. As far as she could see. . . . Her foot flicked the floor button and the switch of headlights gave her a longer and broader but dimmer, more ambered view of the road ahead. The light picked out a round signpost on her right; it said, "S'Agaró." And on her left, wonder of wonders, was a pedestrian, a dark bulk moving toward her on the far side of the narrow road.

She picked up a little speed, just a little, and then wondered about the driver behind her. He seemed to be taking a long time on that descent. She looked up at the mirror—

unnecessarily, since his lights would glaringly announce his presence—and then looked forward again as she heard a shout.

The pedestrian had gone mad.

He was running diagonally across the road and into the path of her car. He was making noises, such loud sounds that she was able to catch an echo of them above the motor, the rain, the sea. His arms were flailing the air like a windmill. There was no time for thought; reflex action jammed her brake pedal to the floor and turned her car's nose toward the sea wall.

But she would hit him; she would inevitably hit him. And she did. She came to a gentle bumping stop, at not quite a right angle to the road, her right fender resting on the sea wall, her left pinning the man against it. And in the next instant, with no gentleness at all, there was a roaring on her left and a car shot past, breath-close—so close that she felt the suction of wind as it pulled at her half-opened window.

Mio's eyes made a slow-motion adjustment as she watched her left front fender crumple, watched the pedestrian cringe away as the new threat brushed past him. The big car crashed into the wall a few feet in front of her, and she saw the shale of the wall lazily rise and fall, most of it into the sea. The car ricocheted back to the road, and went into a descendingly violent series of rockings—to the left of the road, to the right, to the left. Then, fifty feet away, it began to regain its balance. Now, Mio thought, it would stop. She took a deep breath, her first conscious breath in a half minute's time.

The other car righted itself, rolled a few slow feet forward, and then gathered speed and shot ahead. She watched the tail reflector recede into the darkness and then that, too, was gone.

Mio sat motionlessly in her seat and thought of how quiet it seemed. The sea was still crashingly present, and the rain was still thudding on her roof and windshield, but the man-produced violence, the roaring, grinding car had left a vacuum. . . . And then she became aware of a further man-produced disturbance. The pedestrian, still upright, still wedged between her headlights, was imitating a windmill again.

"Oh!" she said. She fumbled at her door handle and called out, "Wait! Are you all right? *Cómo está usted?*" It sounded too social, but her Spanish was not geared to emergencies. She scrambled out into the rain.

The man said, "*No estoy muy bien*. I'm wet. Go back." He motioned violently. "Back up, lady. You are leaning on me. I'm being ground to dust. To mud." He spoke plain American.

She crawled back into her seat, reversed the car, and then pulled up beside him. He pushed himself off the wall, took two limping steps and, grunting, settled into the right-hand front seat. He was enormous, an almost frighteningly big man.

"Hospital," Mio said, "doctor? Where——"

"Not necessary." He shook his big head, and rain spattered out of his close-cut, tightly curled hair. "I'm just crushed. Literally and otherwise. I go for a little walk and look what happens."

The anger that automatically followed her fear swept blazingly over her. "How dare you frighten me like that! What—— Are you crazy? What insanity made you——"

"Hey, wait a minute!"

18

She stopped, not because of the command, but because her fury had pushed her over the border of incoherence and into speechlessness.

"Lady, I saved you. Nobly. I deserve a great reward, the knighting touch of a sword on my shoulder. I——"

A kind of imperturbable good nature came through the darkness toward her, and by its implications of negligent thoughtlessness it infuriated her back into speech. "You saved *my* life? I saved *yours*. If I hadn't swerved, hadn't driven almost into the sea——"

"Yeah, if you hadn't, where would you be now?"

She stared through the darkness at him, feeling again the rush of air as the big car sped past her ear, hearing the roar of its motor. "But," she said, "it—that—his driving, must have been your fault too. He must have been trying to avoid us. Because of you, because——"

"Avoid us? By deserting the straight and narrow to join us on the perimeter?"

She looked blankly at him and saw that his hair was red, so violent a color that it was noticeable even in the dark. She said, "No. I don't know any Spaniards. No one wants to kill me. There could be no reason."

"He wasn't Spanish."

"How could you know that?"

"His license plate——"

"But I remembered to look," she protested. "Before he drove away. I couldn't make the license plate out."

"No, neither could I. It was neatly smeared with mud. But I saw an edge of it. The edge was red."

Red. International license plates were red.

"Now, listen." He turned sideways in his seat and some of the humor left his voice and what she could see of his face.

19

His large rugged features looked boyish but earnest and her impression of thoughtlessness faded. He said, "I was walking along, minding my own business. Your lights came down the hill and as you turned onto the straight, another car rounded the bend up there. First cars I'd seen in a quarter hour of walking. Then, just after you switched your headlights, the other car began to behave in a nutty way. When he reached the lower turn he was a hundred yards or so behind you, yeah? Well, instead of following the road he crossed it, pulled around, and almost stopped. Then he started forward at a nice long angle. And he's got quite a pickup. The maneuver couldn't have been clearer—it was like a man getting ready to break down a door; he backs up, gets into position and then runs dead ahead on target." The follower's lights had not shown in her mirror for what had seemed too long a period, and she had wondered why. This would explain why; he had been on the southbound side of the road, out of focus. "Well, it didn't require much thought on my part. The only way you could avoid that headlong rush would be for you to slow down and veer to your right. So."

"But you took your life in your—— You could have been killed."

"You weren't going very fast. Not much risk."

"Perhaps not from me. Although I *did* touch you. But what about the other car? You were running in front of him too."

He shrugged and the grin returned. "I told you—I'm a hero." He stared out through the rain and added thoughtfully, "Too late to chase him, I suppose."

"Oh yes! *Much* too late."

20

"Well." He shrugged again. "In view of my bruises, could you give me a lift to my hotel?"

"Hotel?"

"Certainly. Where did you think I sprang from, out of the nowhere into the here?"

"I hadn't thought." She put the car into gear. "You are the first pedestrian I've seen since it got dark. I was very—lucky." It seemed an inadequate sentence. "I mean——" She couldn't achieve graciousness. Not yet, because the anger had not passed. "Why didn't he see you?"

"By the time you broadened your lights to include me in, he was angled onto target. Focusing, I suppose. Concentrating."

Fear, fury, incomprehension. She struggled away from them. "Where is your hotel?"

"Quarter mile ahead. Short turn toward the sea. I'll show you."

"Could I eat there?"

"Sure."

"I had hoped to eat dinner in France, but——"

"Long way to go. Very long on a night like this. Midnight."

"Yes. I might even stay in the hotel overnight. Would they—could they accommodate me, do you think?"

He had a rolling laugh. "Lady, lady!" he said. "The hotel is deserted. Naturally; at this time of year the whole coast is deserted. But you're in luck; it's the best hotel between Barcelona and Perpignan. And we can call the police from there."

"No!"

She felt rather than saw the turn of his head.

"I don't like fusses." It didn't seem enough of an explanation. "I don't like to be conspicuous." That was the exact truth, but it wasn't an advance in clarity. "What good would it do?" she asked, aware that she was needlessly saying too much. "We can't describe him or the car. I can't, can you?" She didn't wait for an answer: "They'd just—fuss."

There was a little silence. Then he said, "Well, it's true enough that by the time we get to the cops, or get them to us . . . Still, he had an international license. That would——"

She said firmly, "I'd rather not."

"Entirely up to you, of course."

But after a minute she found the silence uncomfortable. She broke it with a small flanking attack: "I find this coincidence very odd."

"What coincidence?"

"You say the coast is deserted, and yet three Americans—you, me, and the car's driver—all came together on an empty stretch of road."

"Well, now, if you're a collector of coincidences, prepare for more, because there's still another American at the hotel. Actually, the only coincidence lies in your having picked the neighborhood of this hotel for your excitement. You'd be bound to find Americans in the most luxurious joint around. "But"—he looked at her profile—"who said your deadly little pal was American?" She turned her head to stare at him, and he added, "The road, lady, please. Pretend an interest in it."

"*You* said," she protested, looking forward through the rain, "you said——" She stopped.

"Yeah. International license. He could have been a Scotchman or a Greek, no? Unless you happen to know that a fellow countryman of ours has it in for you?"

"No. I told you before——"

"You were talking about Spaniards."

"Because I assumed one met a *Spaniard* on a *Spanish* road. But *no one* wants to kill me. No one!"

"We are not in complete agreement on that point, but I will tactfully drop the subject—— Wait a minute, will you? Pull up ahead there. See him?"

A man was walking toward them, on their right. Mio drove the few yards and stopped.

Her passenger said, "Peter?" and the stranger ducked so that he could put his elbows on the car's edge. In the dark, moon-obscured night Mio could get only a glimpse of his face, but it was enough to startle her somewhat. She looked quickly ahead, and knew her reaction was foolish. The newcomer said, "Hi."

"Did you miss me, Peter? Afraid I'd run off?" The humor in the redheaded man's voice was strong.

The stranger had a contrasting voice—low, slow, lazy. "No," he said. "I was positive you wouldn't go far without me. Just got lonesome, that's all."

"I'll bet. Want a ride back?" He turned to Mio. "May we add to your cargo?"

"Certainly."

The rear door swung open and then closed.

The man beside her said, "My name is Chris Westerland . . . ?"

"Mio Heldon."

"Miss Heldon. And may I introduce Peter Davis, your latest coincidence."

Mio put the car into gear without turning. She said in the direction of the windshield, "How do you do," and they moved forward.

II

THE BLOND ENGLISHMAN—HIS NAME WAS COBHAM
—was finishing a story: "And there I was," he said, "Don
Juan again." He looked like a plump faun.

They all laughed, and Mio found herself thinking that
she was glad she had overcome her first impulse—to have
dinner in her room—and had accepted Mr. Westerland's invitation to join him and his two friends for a cocktail. She
usually found conversation with strangers difficult, and this
evening had seemed to be one of the particularly pointless
byways of life, unplanned, unimportant. She had felt that
she would be a foreign influence—Westerland and the man
they had picked up on the road, Peter Davis, had a peculiar
closeness. They seemed to read each other's minds—like
twin brothers, she thought—and then found the thought
odd. Westerland loomed no smaller and was no less redheaded in the lighted room than he had seemed on the dark
road; Davis's hair was black, and although he was a tallish
man Westerland's bulk belittled Davis's height.

Another reason for her reluctance to venture out into the

world of strangers had been Westerland's insistence on the possibility she preferred to ignore, that someone wished to harm her; the idea made her uncomfortable. And, to be really truthful, she thought, she would have to add that Peter Davis's handsomeness, which she had found so startling when she first glimpsed him through the car's window, continued to throw her even farther than usual into shyness.

But the evening was turning out—so far, at any rate—to be pleasant.

She looked around the room and put the thought into words: "It's nice here," she said. The hotel's bar had those best of barroom qualities, so rarely captured, of warmth and intimacy—small, compact, gleaming, with lighting that revealed everything while maintaining an impression of shadowy dimness. One entire corner was a fireplace, and it was being put to good use.

Peter Davis—he was on her right, the Englishman faced her, and Westerland sat at her left—Davis said, "I suspect it's just the contrast to the cold dark night."

"It's our company." The Englishman looked complacent, caught Mio's eye, and then winked.

"It's the peculiar charm of S'Agaró—of the whole Costa Brava out of season," Westerland told her.

Cobham started the chant: "Us wallahs——"

"Wallowing! . . ."

"In Walachia!" Westerland finished triumphantly, and the three men laughed. That was the third time they had sung out the incomprehensible words. Mio smiled in sympathy with their laughter, but without understanding, and simultaneously decided that Cobham's comment about the charm of the place being caused by the company had a good deal of truth. She said, "That—that running gag escapes me."

"It escapes us too," Cobham assured her, "—at even intervals."

"But what is Walachia?"

"Where, my dear. We're not sure. It was some kind of a country, full of Walachians, and it got a bit lost. Swallowed up by Rumania, I think, and——"

"Hungary or Transylvania," Westerland put in.

Cobham frowned royally. "*And*," he said, overriding interruption, "we keep mentioning it to each other because it reminds us of here. This, too, is a never-never land."

"And the word 'wallah' appeals to us," Davis added in his slow voice. "It sounds so grandly imperial, but Cobham—who swears he's been 'out to the colonies'—says that it's as misleading a term as 'hoi polloi,' that wallah is merely the word for fellow."

"Hoi polloi is misleading because it sounds 'oigh," Cobham explained.

"Oooph!" Chris Westerland bent his big frame in half as if it had sustained a blow in the middle. He let his engaging grin sour slowly.

Cobham smiled sweetly at Westerland and turned back to Mio. "Now that we've got you to help us, Miss Heldon, we're going to do a better job of wallowing. Deeper."

Mio said, "It's Mrs.—Mrs. Heldon."

Cobham's face seemed to be made of firm pink rubber. It had no lines or creases except when he deliberately deflated it. It now went into a sad network of downward grooves. "Ah," he breathed in a sad moan. "And Mr. Heldon will be down at any minute? We have had these fifteen happy minutes of your company merely because you are casing the joint for him?"

"No, I'm a—— Mr. Heldon is dead."

"Oh, I'm sorry." But the pink rubber filled out. "Now that I think of it," he added, "you came in with West and Peter, didn't you?" He smiled genially at her, raised his eyebrows, and kept them there.

There was a second's pause, which Westerland ended. "Mrs. Heldon had a nasty experience. She——" He stopped, looked at Mio, and then said, "Man almost ran into her. I —waved her aside, and so I stand out as a daring, heroic rescuer." Mio saw that the Englishman was following the pauses as carefully as the words. His round face was bland and smiling, but his blue eyes were bright and attentive. She wondered at the intensity of his interest. Westerland added, "And Cobham, before you comment on my luck at being in the right place at the right moment, remember that *I* was courageous enough to go walking in the rain while you softer types cowered indoors."

"Types? But wasn't Peter with you?"

Westerland's big face was expressionless. He said, "We picked him up on the way back."

"Ah? Then this time *Peter* trailed after *you*. I have the darnedest time figuring out who's watching over whom."

Peter Davis said, "You just don't understand the deep roots behind our—attachment."

Mio's shyness submerged itself in her growing interest in whatever was going on behind the words. She turned to look squarely at Davis—the first time she had done so—and found that he was as good-looking as her surprised peeks had threatened. Perfect features, perfectly shaped head covered by a black cap of hair of a kind rarely seen outside of ladies' magazine illustrations. But it was his eyes that accentuated the whole. They were a very pale gray and they provided a startling contrast to his dark skin. The pale eyes were set like a Finn's, high over high cheekbones, and tilted faintly upward. At the moment—at all moments, she realized—his face was without expression, unless laziness were an expression. When he smiled, which wasn't often, the white teeth made the same startling contrast against the tanned skin as did his eyes, but neither smile nor eyes added much warmth. The result wasn't chilling; he merely looked rather remote.

Cobham, too, was staring at Davis. His round face was blank. Mio thought that if, as Davis had said, Cobham didn't understand, he was simply in the same league as she. What, she wondered again, was going on?

Cobham turned back to Mio, and then he abruptly smiled. "Well, then," he said, "here we are!"

"Wallowing," Mio agreed. "And I'm to help. Except that I'll be leaving for France tomorrow, I'd love to help." Out of the growing and, for her, the unusually outgoing curiosity, came her addition: "But what am I to help with?"

There was another small pause. She looked around the table inquiringly. "I mean," she said, "what are you all doing?"

"Speaking for myself," Cobham said, "wallowing. I can't speak for the others. Gentlemen, tell the lady, what are you doing?" There was a clear challenge in his voice. But what, Mio wondered, or who—or why—was he challenging?

Westerland laughed. "Speaking for me, I'm just rolling in peace with you."

"How did you mean, Mrs. Heldon?" Peter Davis asked, his voice quiet against the laughter.

"Why, I had the impression that you were—together. That

28

you were a team of some sort. Engineers, perhaps; something like that."

"I see. No, we're not. I had been here a few days when Cobham came along last week to keep me company. And West blew in three days ago." Three days? she thought. Was she expected to believe that these two men had achieved a twin-brother, two-souls-akin act in three days? But on the other hand, why on earth would they lie about it? Davis added, "And you, Mrs. Heldon, why are you here?"

"Well, it was cold and dark and rutty, and then when that car almost crashed into me the prospect of driving on into France became just too much."

"Peter didn't mean that." Westerland seemed to have no hesitation in interpreting for Davis. "He meant why are you on the Costa Brava in February?"

"Oh." And that was a surprisingly difficult question; at the least, embarrassing. She ducked it. "I suppose I'm just a Walachian."

"Wonderful!" Cobham was openly enchanted. "Citizenship granted. Welcome to our country. And will you dine with us, fellow-Walachian?"

"I'd like to; very much."

"Well, then, let's ask Jaime if we can stay in here. He's the waiter as well as the barman, and I can't see why it should be any more difficult to serve us here. The dining room is immensely drafty."

Jaime was willing. He cleared away the glasses and brought a tablecloth and spread it.

Westerland said, "You'll find dinner quite good, I think, Mrs. Heldon. And I hope you won't mind the company. Cobham is brash, amazingly so for an Englishman, and Davis is terribly quiet, but I'm charming." He tried to look seraphic, and succeeded not at all. But the net result *was* charm, Mio realized.

"Pay no attention to him." Cobham waved Westerland airily into nonexistence. "He has no manners. Davis is handsome, and I strive to make up for his quietness. All this beauty and ebullience makes West jealous. But we'll have a pleasant time in spite of him because we all have got something in common."

A quite pleasant time, Mio agreed silently. "What do we have in common?" she asked.

"Why, we're all wallahs, wallowing——"

Westerland interrupted: "We know, we know. Actually, I think that means a lot."

"What does?" Davis asked.

"Wallahs, wallowing, et cetera, et cetera."

"Why does it mean a lot?" Mio asked obligingly.

Surprisingly, Westerland didn't smile back at her. "Because there can really be no good reason to be any such place at any such time. As witness the emptiness of the whole coast. So any four people who find themselves here must have something in common."

Mio said, without volition but from the depths of a lifelong motivation, "Perhaps we're all running away?"

"From what?" Westerland asked.

The conversation had taken over, and she was dragged reluctantly in its wake. "From ourselves?"

"Tough people to get away from, oneselves." Cobham looked thoughtful and then added, "Something strange about the grammar there."

"Not very British, perhaps." Westerland smiled at him, but the smile didn't have quite its earlier small-boy charm, and altogether some of the charm had left the moment.

30

Jaime served *entremeses*.

Davis broke the contemplative silence: "Maybe you've got a point, West. There can't be any sane reason to be here, unless one just hates people. In that event, you could retire to S'Agaró for half a year with no one to bother you except Jaime."

"I am here for my health." Cobham sounded very firm about it. "Very tender, my health." He saw Mio's smile— she was thinking that he was the rosiest picture of rotund good health she had ever seen—and looked blandly back at her, his small, bright blue eyes very innocent. "And how," he demanded of no one in particular, "could one possibly know whether or not Peter here hates people? Except he's no misogynist." He had caught Peter Davis looking sideways at Mio. Davis surprised her by flushing, and they all laughed.

Davis said, in mock retaliation, "A fine place to be for one's health. It's cold, drafty, damp, and the food swims in fine Spanish olive oil. We'll probably all——" He stopped and the others turned, following his gaze, and saw the man in the doorway.

The man was tall, thin, pale, and less than middle age. His face made an oddly startling impact on those at the table, but only, Mio realized after a second, because of its misplacement in a Latin country. His was a narrow New England face, but without the look of New England grit. The long, thin planes that made the face seemed parsimoniously meager rather than resolutely spare; the narrow, aristocratic nose was intolerant without triumphant righteousness, the thin mouth strangely suggested petulance instead of the tenacity usually inherent in its type. He said, momentary hesitation overlaying what was probably normal arrogance, "I was looking for the dining room." His eyes went from the bar back to their food. "Is this——"

Cobham bounced up. "No," he said, "but we've turned it into one because the dining room is but an open sward. As another American, perhaps you'll join us?" He waved largely at the little table, as if at a bounteous board.

"Why, yes. Good of you," and, formula uttered, the pale man moved forward. There was a general shuffling of chairs as Westerland and Cobham made room between them. Westerland pulled a chair from an adjacent table and pushed it into the space. Mio and Davis remained seated but jockeyed their chairs closer together, and as they did so, Davis said to her in an undertone, "May I bum a ride to France with you tomorrow?"

"Why . . ." There was no reason to say no, but the request was unexpected. And, perhaps only because his voice was so quiet, it had a slight air of furtiveness.

"I would expect to pay my way, of course. Gasoline and so forth."

"Yes, of course you can come along." There was simply no reason to refuse, and she could find no immediate explanation for her feeling of reluctance. He seemed pleasant, but she found his quietness disconcerting; it amounted almost to inanimation. She wondered if he were conserving his energy, and, if so, to what purpose.

He said, "Good." And added surprisingly, "That's a promise?"

The addition strongly increased her reluctance. But there was no polite way out. "Yes."

The newcomer ended the side exchange by saying to Cobham, "But are *you* American?"

"Sometimes," Westerland said before Cobham could

answer. "He has an amazing command of the language, at any rate. The rest of us are American beyond question. My name is Westerland."

"Peter Davis," Davis said. "And this is Mrs. Heldon."

The stranger sat down and stared at Mio. "Jones," he announced. "Arthur Jones." He made a stiff little bow.

Davis smiled without obvious reason. He asked, "And what are you doing in S'Agaró, Mr. Jones? Are you here for a rest?"

"For my health," said Mr. Jones, and looked entirely unamused at the general laugh that followed. He raised affronted eyebrows.

Cobham sobered, settled into his chair, and passed the sad-looking remainder of the *entremeses* to Jones. "Just use the platter, we've finished. My name is Jim Cobham, and you're quite right about me; I'm an Englishman—although Chris here constantly flatters me by seeming to doubt my regretful disclaimer of the land where gold lies on the streets. . . . Do excuse us for laughing, but you came in on a tag. *I* had just claimed to be here for my health, and I was told that it was balderdash. Or words to that effect."

"It had been suggested that we must all be fleeing from something," Davis elaborated.

"Or from someone," Westerland added.

"But that won't hold, old boy," Cobham said earnestly, "because, the Good Book to the contrary, I don't believe that the wicked flee when no man pursueth, or maybe I just believe that the pursuers have got more get-up-and-go than they did in Biblical days."

"Get-up-and-go?" Westerland muttered with a quizzical half-smile. "Is that an Anglicism?" Cobham did an elaborate business of ignoring him. Westerland's smile grew and then

33

faded. He added, "So you mean that if some of us are fleers, others must be pursuers?"

"It would follow, wouldn't it?" He gave Westerland the sweetly innocent smile that seemed to be the insult added to the injury of his puns.

For a moment there was a complete but not unfriendly silence. If some of the charm had gone from the room and the hour, Mio thought, what filled the void was not enmity, one for the other, but an acceptance of enmity on the part of the world. The continuing air of conspiracy, of undertone, of padded darts, thickened but did not sharpen. The three men were not together, not sharing an enterprise, so they had said, but they *were* increasingly together in their apartness. Mio examined that thought and decided that in a confused way it expressed her partial comprehension.

Davis spoke as from that bond of three to the outsider in their midst. "And you, Mr.—Jones," he asked, "are you a fleer or a pursuer?"

Jones was a man who would normally be colorless, as if an assurance of superiority were so clearly implicit in him that any display of personality would be vulgarly redundant, but at that moment sheer indignation had tinted him pink and had given him a little force. "Really!" he said in a tone caught between outrage and fussiness. "I am here for my health. I——" He choked.

Mio watched the pink rise in his sallow face and discovered something unexpected. Mr. Arthur Jones's long, attenuated features were rather too regular and too abortively ascetic, and his sandy color was uninteresting, but by basic definition he was a good-looking man. Her sudden laugh was a gay, tinkling sound and, issuing from a face so serene and withdrawn, it always took those who heard it for the first time by surprise. Four pairs of eyes moved to her face.

"Fleeing or pursuing," Westerland murmured, "we're a happy bunch." He smiled crookedly in sympathy with Mio's continuing ripples of laughter. "Let us in on it?"

"Perhaps it's a joke that only women would understand." Her eyes were still smiling, and that was not usual; hers was an extraordinarily still face. "But, you see, we women go on searches—searches for presentable escorts. We take summer cruises, winter cruises, and just cruises. We go to beaches, mountaintops, and lakes, always in season, of course. We even take courses in mechanical engineering and printing administration—because women are so logical and those are logical places to find presentable men. Reverting to your flee-and-pursue quote, Mr. Cobham, it is known that we, the not so wicked, flee only after we have made very certain that there are pursuers around. Well, the point is that here I am in one of the world's least populated spots, about as out of season as one can get, and I find myself surrounded by four extremely attractive men."

"Are you including *me*?" Cobham asked, beaming, but patting his small rotundity deprecatingly.

"You have all the appeal, Mr. Cobham, of a small boy who has been a bit too often to the jam pot, but gets away with it through sheer charm."

"Now, there, Cobham!" Westerland was grinning widely. "That is as turned by a master."

"And sincere, too," Cobham assured him. "In reward for your sagacity and discernment, Mrs. Heldon, you may call me Jim. Or anything else you wish—preferably 'darling.' And I will go one step further and assure you that I, as a widower, *am* eligible. Probably more than my fellow-Adonises can say."

"I am a bachelor, Mrs. Heldon." Westerland leaned across the table and added confidentially, "Far more eligible than a widower."

"Not a bit of it. It is well known that women find widowers better trained." Cobham achieved a look of insufferable smugness, and Mio laughed again.

Davis said, "I agree with Chris. I am a bachelor too," he told Mio gravely.

Westerland said, "Well, Mr. Jones? Declare yourself."

"I am divorced," Jones said stiffly.

"Tch, tch." Westerland's face took on a look of pained distress. "Who would have thought it?"

"Ineligible," Cobham pronounced. "As bad, by reputation, as widowers are good. Divorcés have *proved* they can't take it. However, Mrs. Heldon—what *is* your first name, since we are practically engaged?"

"Hermione. They call me Mio."

"Lovely. Well, Mio, there is a flaw in all this. It is with reluctance but an unerring sense of fairness that I must so advise you."

"The almost-engaged state has brought a rare pomposity to Jim. Can't you see how impossibly dull he'd be around the house?" Westerland asked Mio.

Cobham ignored him. He said to Mio, "These researching ladies you have explained to us go not only where they may hope to find gents, but they have the further hope that the gents will prove eligible. That they will return from Brighton or the Isle of Man to being solicitors' clerks or drapers' assistants. Even, perhaps, to being solicitors or drapers—depending upon luck. The lucky ones get the drapers. These lads have got suitable mums and dads, maybe even suitably dead mums and dads. And bachelor digs in Maida Vale. All that. Whereas when a lady dabbles in the out-of-season the chances are rum, if you see what I mean. She can no longer be sure that her gentlemen will have an *in*-season. She doesn't know who they are or whence they come."

"Or what they've done," Westerland murmured.

"Precisely," Cobham said. He put a stubby forefinger in the center of the tablecloth and tapped it once. His face was entirely grave. "Or what they've done," he repeated.

III

Dinner was over when Ibáñez came.

The conversation had taken a further odd twist, and Mio, in her fascinated desire to untangle what was going on, had almost lost her self-consciousness. She listened silently as the men, particularly Jim Cobham and Chris Westerland, discussed the Astra Armored Car robbery of a few years before. The discussion had an incongruous heat, and Mio got the startled impression that there was something personal in it. Were they—for God's sake—highway robbers? Were they (her mind did not always obey—whose does?—and it now permitted an undesirable seepage) were they, or, excluding Westerland, one of the other three, responsible for her near-mishap? And at that, it could have been a four-way conspiracy. Westerland's heroic gesture could have been a decoying tactic, a—— The thought was so fantastic that it was easy to shut off. She returned her attention to the conversation.

"I still say"—Westerland sounded dogged—"it was clever."

"Clever, clever!" Cobham threw up his hands. "A minute ago you said 'masterful'——"

"I didn't use that word."

"Well, something that implied that word. And *I* still say —clever, but only to a point. Clever in conception, if you like. Clever in execution, if you like, but——"

"If I like! Over a million and a quarter dollars disappeared into limbo. There wasn't a single witness, since the four men in the armored car were found dead—mysteriously dead, as I remember it: not shot, garroted, knifed. I don't think the papers ever explained the manner of their dying. If they did, I never read it. Did you?"

"No, but——"

Westerland didn't wait. "Maybe they took poison?" He accompanied the sarcasm with a polite lift of his eyebrows. "They stopped their car on a deserted country road and accepted one cup of hemlock apiece? Why, there was even a report that there were no tire prints on the road, and no footprints except those in an immediate, very small radius of the car. And it hadn't rained. Perhaps they all got out with brooms and swept a half mile of road?" He paused, and then added scornfully, "Clever—if *I* like!"

"Well"—Davis's indolent voice had a peacemaking note— "there *were* those footprints you mentioned, weren't there?"

"Yeah, and do you remember about them?" Westerland turned animatedly toward Davis, but got only a headshake in response. "They were *identical!* First everyone seemed to think one guy had done all the work, and then they realized that the prints were in different sizes—four or five sets of 'em. But somebody had been clever enough to equip the group with brand-new identical sneakers that left a distinct pattern —and that are sold in the United States in quantities of something like a million pairs a year. I wouldn't call that a slip from the level of genius. *You* tell me, Peter—don't *you* think it was clever?"

"I simply don't know enough about it."

"You must have an opinion."

"I don't, though." Davis sounded bored.

Mio's dark eyes swiveled from Westerland to Davis. The aggressive challenge in Westerland's voice was a jarring contrast to his previous good-natured acceptance, seemingly of all things. Why should he attempt to force Davis into expressing an opinion on a matter so remote from S'Agaró? And it seemed such a fruitless attempt: Davis was unlikely to be forced into anything whatever. He remained lazy, unconcerned, unperturbed.

The genial Cobham had lost his smile; Mio thought that he shared her confusion. "West," he said, breaking the deadlock, "there was another thing I found beautifully intriguing—like that one mysterious clue around which Agatha Christie builds such lovely puzzles. Out on the road the authorities picked up three long wavy blond hairs, stuck together at the ends. Remember?"

"Now, that sounds easy enough to figure," Davis offered lazily. "Simply a false mustache. Something like that."

Cobham laughed. "In your inimitable vernacular, Oh yeah? A mustache over six inches long?"

"Oh. Well, false beard?"

"Same answer."

"Toupee? Or simply someone's own hair?"

"Do you know anyone whose hair comes in clumps of three and who wears it seven inches long?"

"Not personally," Davis admitted. He considered. He seemed to have been intrigued into the discussion by Cobham in a way that Westerland's forcefulness had failed to accomplish. He said, "How about its having belonged to a girl?"

"The shoe sizes were too big."

Davis smiled. "You should know some of the girls I know. Personally. But I suppose you're right. No good reason for getting a woman into such a job, anyway. Unless—maybe she was an Annie Oakley?"

"Who was shot?"

"Um." Davis visibly retired from the competition.

Westerland's urgency seemed to have receded. Now he laughed and said, "There is something I find even more intriguing than the three hairs, Jim, and that is your great knowledge of the case. Tell me, did the London *Times* report our local robbery in column after column of infinite detail?"

Cobham smiled sweetly at him. "My dear fellow," he said, "I wouldn't have the least idea. I wasn't in London at the time. I was in the States."

"Checkmate!" Westerland's ready laugh rolled out.

"But so easy, old boy! So much easier to explain your little confusion about my knowledge than to explain the three hairs. But look now: before you get back into the details, let me finish the sentence I started ten minutes ago, because it changes the whole point of view. I was all for admitting that the whole affair was handled cleverly from the angles of conception and execution, but what I wanted to know was what happened to the money?"

Westerland stared at him. "Happened to it? They stole it."

"Yes, yes. But are they using it?"

"Well, they aren't making paper dolls of it."

"Ah, but I suggest you may be wrong in that surmise. To use stolen money in quantities is not easy. Not in *quantities*. Paper dolls may now look to them like the only way to cut ducks and drakes. Do you realize how much physical space such an amount of money would displace?"

"Well"—Westerland looked thoughtful—"a bill is a little more than two and a half inches wide and a little more than six inches long. It is point oh oh four three inches thick, so a packet one inch thick comprises two hundred and thirty-three notes. We could work it out, but we'd be guessing at the denominations."

There was a startled silence, and then Jones cleared his throat and decided to descend to conversation. "That's an amazing little display of knowledge, sir," he said.

"Why?" Westerland, bewildered, looked engagingly small-boyish. "Anyone with a six-inch ruler can find two of the dimensions. And as for the thickness, well, the facts are printed in a hundred places."

"Perhaps so." Jones looked unconvinced. "*I've* never read them."

"Done you there, West!" Cobham was displaying his plump-faun grin. "*I've* never read them either."

"You"—Westerland's voice was heavy with irony—"are an Englishman."

"Indeed I am. But I've never read such facts about English bank notes, either. I can only say that they would be thicker than yours. They have an air of solidity."

"An *air*," Chris commented.

"Are you an Anglophobe, old boy? And so fond of me you're trying to claim me for the States? Getting back to the thickness. Suppose we take your figures——"

"But let's get back to the matter of cleverness." Davis's

low voice was unexpected. They all turned toward him. "Couldn't it have been largely a matter of luck?"

"No." Westerland sounded very positive. "You read the papers. Did it read like luck to you?"

"There wasn't really very much in the papers, you know. Not about the details, the actual workings of the business. As you yourself said, they never even revealed the cause of the men's deaths." Davis wasn't being argumentative but merely making an observation. "All right, then, say they were clever. Wouldn't they then have been clever enough to figure out how to dispose of the money? I mean, how to make it spendable?"

"Now there," said Westerland, "there you have a point. He could—they could—"

"Señora. Señores."

They had all looked up, and Mio thought the others were startled, too, as she was. The room was so small, so intimate, it seemed impossible for anyone to have arrived at their table's edge without being noticed. But the man had something of the quality of a shadow. He was small and, of course, dark. (Where were the blond Spaniards one constantly heard of?) He was dressed entirely in black, except for—again "of course"—white socks. His face was an anonymous collection of conventional features. Mio felt that if she passed him in the hallway in fifteen minutes' time she would not recognize him. He said again, "Señora. Señores."

"Yes," Cobham said. "Yes, señor? Can we do something for you?"

The little man looked gratified. "Yes," he said. "Just that. To do something for me would be so kind of you." He put his hand on a chair back at the next table and made a small pulling gesture toward them. The dark eyebrows rose in expressive inquiry.

"Certainly," Cobham answered. "Do sit down."

The Spaniard sat on the edge of the chair, and the five looked blankly at him, waiting. "My name," he said carefully, "is Ibáñez. This is a little formality, and I thought it might be more easy, more pleasant, if I came here to see you. More pleasant than if you were to come to—to our office. And I can see you all. All at once. All the strangers, that is. You see, you are all the strangers, the visitors, in S'Agaró. At the *pensions* there is no one. The season, you know. So you see."

Mio looked involuntarily at her watch and thought that she did not see. It was ten-forty at night, an odd time to—to do what?

Cobham said, "Your office, señor? What office is that?"

The little man hesitated. Then he said, "The office of the Guardia Civil. The local office."

The Guardia Civil, Mio thought—one of the police forces. The national one. Like the FBI. No, she corrected herself; more like the SS or the OGPU. But they always wore those funny-looking patent-leather hats like Napoleon's, and they came in pairs—like doves. Or vultures. Did vultures come in pairs? She tried to straighten out her thinking: If he didn't wear a uniform, presumably he was a higher official.

Arthur Jones leaned across the table and said in his dry, haughty voice, "What can the police want with us? Or is it just one of us?"

"Just a little inquiry. Of all strangers. And I, of the Guardia, come as—as an accommodation to the passport people. It is a passport matter. Just a formality."

"But," Cobham said, "I showed my passport and filled

out the police form at the hotel desk, as one always does. As I presume my companions did?" He looked around the table and the others nodded. "So—there is more?"

"Just a little formality." The Spaniard had black gloves of thin suède, rather like a woman's gloves, which he was holding in his lap. He twisted them in mute distress. "There has been some irregularity, and because we are interested in—in someone else, of a certainty—we would like to see your passports. *Norteamericanos*, citizens of the United States, are so welcome here—and of Great Britain, of course." He bowed hastily at Cobham. "We would not want that you misunderstand."

Mio had a sick feeling at her stomach. That *paella*, she thought, and knew that the *paella* had nothing to do with it. Though a mist of discomfort she saw Peter Davis reach inside his suit jacket and bring forth the familiar olive-green booklet. Davis said, "Well, if you want to see our passports, there needn't be any fuss about it. As I understand the Spanish regulations, you are entitled by your law to see them whenever you wish." He held out the passport, and the Spaniard took it gratefully.

There was silence while he examined the front pages. Then he closed the booklet and returned it to Davis. His voice was expressionless: "Ah yes. Mr. Davis. We have had dealings with you before, no?"

"No," Davis said, his face and low voice outdoing the Spaniard's in expressionlessness. "Not to my knowledge."

"You were involved in the death of the American at Tossa de Mar, down the coast, no?"

"No," Davis said again. "I was at Tossa de Mar when an acquaintance died. Of heart failure. There was no question of involvement."

"Ah, my English, it is not good," the Spaniard said easily. "I merely meant that I had heard your name." His eyes moved counterclockwise and stopped at Westerland. "*Señor, por favor?* You have your passport with you?"

Westerland didn't answer. He had a peculiar expression on his face, a look almost of curiosity. He reached for and presented a passport.

The Spaniard took it with his little bow, and again went gravely through the first pages. "Chris-to-*pher* West-er-*land*," he enunciated. His eyes came up. "Tourist," he added. He returned the book. "Thank you." He looked at Jones.

Jones handed over his passport with an air of humoring the canaille. "Ah yes, señor." Ibáñez showed a small animation. "This is one of the very minor irregularities. You have signed on the police form that your profession is *abogado*—lawyer, you say? Barrister?"

"Lawyer," Cobham advised him. He looked amused.

"*Gracias.* . . . As lawyer. But the passport does not so say, no?"

"No." Jones was oddly taken aback, his air of condescension clouded over with an uncharacteristic confusion. "No," he repeated, "of course it doesn't. That is—well, you know, just force of habit. Force of—— It doesn't matter, does it?"

"Why, no, señor. As long as you do not here practice law. But then you could not do so anyway, could you? In Spain, I mean." He smiled and said, "And you, señora?"

Mio's black eyes looked very large. She was staring at Jones with an intensity that left no room for Ibáñez. A lawyer who was not a lawyer, and his name was Arthur Jones.

"Señora?"

46

Her eyes swung back to the Spaniard's face, her small face blank of expression; only the deepening whiteness showed her tenseness. "Oh," she said. "Oh yes. My passport." She reached into her purse and pulled it out, but she didn't move it toward him. "Señor, may I ask—— Is it illegal——" She stopped, hesitated, and then handed over the passport.

The *guardia* seemed as fascinated by her face as she had been by Jones's. After a minute he cleared his throat, looked down at the passport, and said, "Ah yes. Señora—Heldon. This is another small irregularity reported by the clerk of the desk. He reported your—request. It is not, as you say, illegal, but it is—irregular, no?"

She nodded almost imperceptibly, her eyes fastened on his face. He returned the gaze and then with an air of decision snapped the book shut and returned it. He said to Cobham, almost abruptly, "And you, señor?"

"Yes?" Cobham was looking at Mio, and his expressive face seemed to be caught between amusement and concern.

"Your passport."

"Oh, of course." He put his hand inside his jacket and said to Westerland, "Now you'll have a chance to see that I carry a plain dark blue affair, none of your fancy green swirls. Shades of our preoccupation with the Navy, perhaps. . . . Dear me, it's in my room." He stood up. "If you'll wait a sec, Señor Ibáñez, I'll bring it right down." He moved jauntily through the doorway.

Davis said, obviously bridging the moment, "We are really the only tourists in S'Agaró, señor?"

"The season." The Spaniard was deprecating. "For nine months we have many people, naturally, but in winter . . ." He shrugged.

"You remind me," Westerland said brightly, "of the California officials. There it never rains."

"Indeed?" The Spaniard didn't understand, but Mio saw the little joke. Ibáñez had increased the livable months on the coast from six to nine. And she also understood that her embarrassment must be obvious and that the two men were making conversation to rescue her from it. Her eye caught Jones's and she was startled by his expression. He, too, evidently found her predicament interesting, but less amiably so. He had stared at her, she realized, from the moment he entered the room, but what had been behind the stare was clearer now: a kind of fascination mixed with enmity. But— enmity? Granted that he was the same Jones, that did not presuppose . . .

He said, "So your name is Heldon, madam?" It wasn't mere enmity; it was venom, and unmistakable.

Before she could formulate an answer to the attack, Westerland said, "Why, yes. You were introduced to Mrs. Heldon an hour ago. Had you forgotten?"

Mio was remotely grateful, and then cold anger displaced both fear and gratitude. "Yes," she said, "Heldon. And you, Mr. Jones, you are a lawyer? Or aren't you?"

Jones's pale venom developed a murderous intensity. "I should think, madam——" he started, but a scraping sound interrupted him; Ibáñez's chair had grated on the floor boards as he pushed it back and rose.

"Where is the Señor Cobham's room?" he asked sharply.

There was a startled pause. Then Westerland drawled, "You would have to ask the desk clerk that question."

"Yes. Excuse me." The little man was out of the room faster than Mio would have believed possible, and Jaime, the bartender, left on his heels, spouting Catalan, an odd-sounding mixture of Valencian and Provençal, with touches of Arabic, which Mio had never attempted to master.

Davis said to Westerland, "You know where Cobham's room is."

"Sure. So do you. Right at the top of the stairs."

There was a pause.

Then Westerland started to laugh. "Skipped, by God!" he choked. "He beat it out! And a beautiful job of it, too. Sat right there through the whole business, went into the bluff as neatly as I've ever seen it done, and then he skipped. So he was the one!"

Jones said stiffly, "If they were looking for an Englishman and that—gentleman—was the only Englishman present, I can't see why we were all subjected to inquiry."

"Perhaps they were looking for someone else, too." Davis clearly didn't like Arthur Jones. Mio was surprised that his inanimation could relax enough to permit even as pale an emotion as dislike.

Westerland was still convulsed. "And all Jim's pregnant comments about what we've done and where we came from weren't nearly as appropriate as where we are going to. Because where he's going to seems far more to the point. Poor guy!"

"Why so poor?" Davis asked indifferently.

"Why, if his passport is suspect it'll be no cinch to get out of the country."

"But he was right," Mio said slowly. The lethal attack on her on the dark road (for it had, of course, been an attack —just that); the possibility that one of these men had been responsible for it—because there was that international license plate and they were "the only strangers" in S'Agaró; the weird, puzzling conversation; the contretemps of the passport; the knowledge that these men—at the very least, one of these men—"went into bluffs, and skipped"—all combined to overwhelm and exhaust her. "He was quite right," she said, "because where we come from and what we've done determine how far and how fast we run." She stood up. "Doesn't it?" she asked. No one answered. "If you'll excuse me," she said, "I'll go to bed. Good night."

IV

A PEASANT WAS SITTING BY THE ROADSIDE. LARGE black *sombrero*, *chaqueta* and all, he didn't look Spanish. That was what came of leaping to conclusions, she thought. All Spaniards were dark, hm? Saturnine? Thin? Bustling? This man was asleep, his wide hat almost resting on his chin and showing the blond hair on the back of his head. And why shouldn't he be tired? Mio thought wearily. It was barely 7 A.M.

Her horn drew a surprised attendant.

She asked for gasoline.

"*Sí, señora!*" He stared at her for a full minute and then said, "*Sí, sí, sí, sí, señora!*" He ran toward the garage, probably to get the keys to the pump, staring over his shoulder at her with such oblivious fascination that he ran full tilt into the doorframe.

Serves him right, Mio thought. So Spanish ladies aren't out of their *casas* at this hour. Spanish ladies don't drive cars. In fact Spanish *women* don't drive cars. But, she thought, if you're attending a gas pump on this single,

Godforsaken track, my friend, you've certainly seen the mad foreign señoras—even señoritas, *por dios!*—chauffeuring themselves before now. But not, her mind added in fairness, at this hour.

The sight of her could apparently raise the almost-dead— the *payés* had lifted his head. He said conversationally, "Hallo, ducks!" He unfolded, not without effort, and came to the car window. "Thought you'd be ridin' this way, pardner."

Mio stared at him, her face serene but her interior in the uproar that a shock always created in her. She had long ago learned to conceal the outer evidences of her too ready and too intense flurries of fright, but the effort invariably threw her into sarcasm or anger. After the minute of adjustment she said bitterly, "Why don't you get your idiom straight?"

He looked exaggeratedly chastened. "You don't think my drawl goes with my hat?"

"Maybe your drawl does, but your figure doesn't. I thought you were never going to get your stomach off that bank."

"Tummy, ducks. Stomach is a naughty word."

"Only in England. Correct your idiom; not mine."

He looked at her with an odd sympathy. Then he said, "See you down the road, ducks. Two minutes." He ambled off, northward.

Five minutes later Mio rounded the bend and squealed to a vicious stop. Cobham had sunk down on another bank. He rose wearily and limped to the car's side. He surveyed her casually and then reached thoughtfully into a pocket of his *pantalón* and brought out a wrist watch. "Well," he said. "Early. So you're on the lam, huh?"

Mio spluttered.

Cobham smiled. "Look, ducks——"

"Stop calling me 'ducks'! What's all this?"

"All what?"

"To start with, the outfit."

"Oh, this is a little thing I—uh—picked up."

"You stole it."

"You are developing a most unbecoming fascination with words and titles, madam."

"What are you doing here?"

"Waiting for you, ducks. Uh—madam."

"Don't call me 'madam'!"

"Words, words! Shall I go back into character and call you ma'am? Or perhaps—Mrs. Heldon?"

There was silence on the quiet road. Then Mio said, "If you're looking for help, that's no way to ingratiate yourself."

"Oh? I'm to plead?"

Mio looked into his tired face and found no trace of humor there. She said slowly, "Why, no. No, I didn't mean that."

The full face developed a small, weary smile. "Sorry. I'm tired. Been walking in these half the night." He held up a foot, exhibiting one of his ill-fitting, rope-soled, canvas-topped *alpargatas; espardenyas,* the Catalans called them. "I say, drive in there, will you? In among that clump of trees. The sight of an *estrangera* and a *payés* talking together on the edge of nowhere would startle even the mules that patrol this road."

Mio hesitated. This was the man who bluffed and fled. This——

"—unless you're afraid," he added. His face was sober.

Mio said, "No." Then unaccountably she said, "No," again, and piloted the Citroën over the bank. She drove fifty feet, maneuvered until she couldn't be seen from the road, and cut the motor. Cobham crawled in beside her on the front seat and let out a sigh. "Well, fellow-fleer, how goes it?"

"I wish——" She stopped, and started again. "I'm not a fleer, you know."

"No?"

"Not the way you mean it."

"Not from the authorities?" His face, in repose, was very shrewd. "Just a fellow-Walachian, then? Wallowing in the hope of obscurity?"

"I—— If you insist."

"I insist, my dear, for an entirely practical reason. If you are among the real living, if you live each day to its fullest, if you flee from no more than most people—just a memory or two—well, then . . . I mean, if you are moving with a destination, if—— Where are you heading?"

"Now? Perpignan, and then Paris."

"Well, if Perpignan holds friends who are waiting for you, if Paris holds a lover, or if it's a port to home and friends and family, then I won't say any more."

It was quiet in the little glade. It would, for February, be a warm day—perhaps reach fifty degrees. A bird or two found it delightfully invigorating. The trees were scrubby, and probably the view was barren, but the sun had not yet dispelled the ground mist and the landscape was mysterious with promise. If you didn't know better, Mio thought. She said, "Say any more . . . ?"

"Is that an answer?"

"Yes. Paris is not a port to anywhere."

"Ah." A stranger would not consider his an actor's face, Mio thought. He looked, at first sight, merely good-natured.

But, by the mysterious rearrangement of the smallest lines, his face could be infinitely expressive. Now two minute depressions had aligned themselves beside his mouth, and the sadness was there to see. "Well," he said—and miraculously became all gay. "Well! Then we're off!"

Mio raised her eyebrows. "Are we really? To Perpignan?"

"No, no, my pigeon! South."

"South? Then why did you come north?"

"Because they expected me to go south."

"Then why do you want to go south?"

"Because by now they've decided I've gone north."

"I think we had better go a little slower. In fact, let's go back to the beginning: Why did they expect you to go south in the first place?"

"Because it was too obvious that the nearest ways out— Port-Bou, Bourg-Madame, even San Sebastián and from there by boat to St. Jean-de-Luz or Biarritz—were all to the north. I would think that was too obvious, and I would go south. See?"

"Dimly. All right, now they have decided you were too smart and you have come north. Won't they take the next step and realize that you'll now go south?"

"Ducks, I am an Englishman."

Mio stared at him, and then the pleasant tinkling sound that was her laugh rose in the glade. "And if you were Spanish?"

"Spanish, they'd make three revolutions more and look north. American, two twists and south. French, one more turn and they'd rush northward. That's a lovely laugh, my dear Mio, but, once heard, never forgotten. You had better restrain it from now on. You may smile at me constantly."

She smiled at him.

"I'll never understand American women. Thank God, I suppose. But you should look Spanish, you know. All that heavy, straight, inky-black hair. Your eyes. Even the fair skin —extremely Castilian. Most of all, that look of complete serenity. But somehow you are indelibly American. Of course, your nose is by no means patrician enough."

"Bad?"

"Undeniably pug. And your teeth are crooked."

"You noticed that?"

"Inevitably."

"Sad, isn't it?"

"Not heartbreaking. I just want you to know that I see through you. That *I* know you're not the beauty you go bluffing people into thinking you are. I shall remind myself of it constantly."

She smiled at him. "I could tell the Spanish a thing or two about you."

"I fervently hope you won't. What?"

"That you do other things than flee better than they'd think. That was quite the nicest. Far better than the Spanish. They sound all formula."

"Garn!" he said, and abruptly, small-boyishly, he resembled Chris Westerland. Ten years and thirty pounds off, and about three inches on . . . He said, "Let us be all sensible-like and make plans."

"The grove is yours."

"I grieve to make the grove grave." He saw her face and stole her thought. "Your disgust with my—wit—reminds me of West. Well, now—we go south. We go by road for the lovely reason that this nice little Citroën isn't a goat. We go by *this* road because there is no other except the Gerona route, and that would be adding unnecessary mileage and danger to reach a neighborhood equally patrolable."

"And *where* would you have us go?"

"To Barcelona . . . You don't like that?"

"I have just spent three months there."

"Ah. Lovely city, isn't it? But a bit dull this time of year, I admit. Let's pray that it will continue to be so. No excitement, please heaven. We go to Barcelona because it's the best and nearest port to Majorca, or perhaps Ibiza. Anchored somewhere around in the Baleares is a dissolute but entirely honest friend of mine. In his yacht. A fancy thing, it is. Sleeps ten. Room for fifty at a good party, so there will be fifty aboard. At least. I shall get lost in the crowd. It's a bit of sheer luck that no one about happens to know Tony and I went to school together. He will pilot me out of this charming country. He will ask no questions—raise his eyebrows, perhaps—and no one would dream of asking him any; Tony is a milord."

"Mr. Cobham——" He stared at her with exaggerated astonishment. She smiled slightly but didn't correct the form of address. "Mr. Cobham, it would not be very—well, intelligent of me to go chauffeuring you around, now would it?"

"No," he said promptly.

"Well, then." She spread her hands, and thought that it was ridiculous to feel ungracious.

There was a quiet minute. Then Cobham said, "It would not be intelligent, but it would probably not be actually dangerous, either. As an American, you could plead off any trouble. Look innocent, and all that. At the absolute worst they would pop you out of the country, and you were going anyway, no?"

She looked at him silently.

"As for danger from me—I am a lamb. Lancelot gone to fat. Famous for it. Lambhood, that is; not fat. I am a true Englishman, fair play, the proper regard taught me at my——" He stopped abruptly, and then his voice, in her short experience a matter of ups, downs, inflections, unexpected pitches, became astonishingly level: "I offer you my word that you will come to no harm through me personally."

Even on a level plane the voice achieved expressiveness. And the expression, Mio realized with an odd sense of shock, was wistfulness. Without further thought she said, "I accept that pledge. Okay, I am your chauffeur."

Cobham became Cobham. "Sensible girl! Ah, wrong word, sensible, huh? But there's something else, you know."

"There's what else?"

"Gotta get up and go. Adventure is good for people. You don't want to stagnate."

"No?" She found it an uncomfortable bit of insight. "Well, I suggest that this particular adventure may well be doomed from the start. Will no one raise an eyebrow at *una estrangera y un campesino* traveling happily together at the wrong time of year in generally the wrong direction?"

"Elementary. I shall be on the floor in the rear of this palatial vehicle."

"If I ever had any doubts, which I didn't, I would have just lost them: West to the contrary, you are *not* American."

"How did I give myself away?"

"All American boys, even well-brought-up ones, came home from the wars saying vee-*hick*-ul."

"Ah?" His face became expressionless. "*Not* Q.E.D.—I didn't march to the wars. So—let's toodle."

"A question first, please. How in the world did you find me?"

"I didn't find you; I waited for you. Look, ducks: Anyone who starts along this road soon realizes that petrol stations are about as plentiful as honest men. So he grasps the first opportunity. As you did."

"And you knew I *would* start along this road?"

"Yes, Mio."

She knew she shouldn't ask. "How?"

"My dear, I think you're afraid of something. That you panic, and run. You've got a lovely serene mask, all Madonna-like, but underneath . . . I'm curious about one thing: how do you know so much about the Spaniards' line of blarney?"

She flushed. "You think they wouldn't say anything nice to me?"

"I think you wouldn't stand still long enough. 'A startled doe' is not very original, but it occurs forcibly to me."

"Well, they *begin* floridly."

"Ah!" He nodded. "You should really try slowing up for finishes once in a while. Compliments—laid floridly before you like a lane of rose petals—could almost make a path out of Walachia."

"Jim, if I look—serene, how do you—why do you think I'm afraid?"

"Fellow-Walachian. Siblings under the skin. Kipling. All that. I recognize like; I'm afraid too." He paused. "Well," he said, and got out of the car and opened the back door.

She had known she shouldn't ask; she hadn't wanted to hear. But it had been less painful than she feared, and as valueless as she suspected. She said brightly, "You've forgotten something."

"Cobham the Great? Impossible." He climbed into the back.

"If I tour calmly south, won't I create quite a flutter in a neighborhood already aflutter? They know I went north. On the hotel police form I gave my destination as Paris. I even asked about the road. So how do we get me through to Barcelona unsearched?"

"We don't. Always, in your career as fleer, you must bow to the inevitable. But as you bend into your bow you grasp said inevitable firmly and twist it a bit." The car swayed as he plumped himself on the floor. "Tight fit," he said. "Now, ducks, onto the road and off. *I* have a destination, the largest port on the Inland Sea. I shall explain en route how we will twist the inevitable. *Vamos!*"

Mio started her motor, briefly regretted disturbing the peaceful grove, and backed bumpily out, to the accompaniment of appropriately placed grunts of minor agony from Cobham. She said, "Shut up, Jim. This is the merest beginning. The road itself is even worse, you know."

He groaned more loudly. "I do know. Wonder how Hannibal felt about it?"

"Hannibal?"

"Trod this road during his march on Rome."

"Maybe he *caused* the ruts." She gained the road, faced the car southward, and started. As she passed the gas station, she asked, "And Jim, why are you fleeing?"

"Oh, that. I'm a thief."

V

MIO WENT THROUGH THE SHORT STRETCH THAT WAS
S'Agaró at a steady twenty-five, which was not fast enough
to interfere with her view of the faces—that of the astonished
cop lounging in the *plaza*, whose mouth dropped open; the
face of the man, draped over a barrel in front of the *bodega*,
who straightened up abruptly and started off in the opposite
direction as she passed him; she even saw Luis, who had
carried her baggage the night before from her car to her
room, and who now did a beautifully timed, head-swinging
double take. Mio moved on steadily, seeming to see no one,
for about a hundred yards, or until she had reached the
southernmost edge of the village; there she stopped and
parked in front of a café. The car stood out on the quiet
street with the splendid ostentation of the solitary. She examined the café. The tiny tables outside looked forlorn, but
it was growing warm. . . . She decided it would be pleasant
enough and even more conspicuous outside. Above almost
anything on earth Mio disliked being conspicuous, but she
was always thorough. Her job here was to be seen; she would

therefore be well seen. She put her head through the doorway, said to the man behind the counter, "*Café negro? Fuera, por favor,*" and then chose a centered table and waited.

The thimbleful of coffee and Ibáñez arrived together, Ibáñez's arrival being the more noticeable. All her impressions of quietness and shadows disappeared as Ibáñez sped down the quiet street in a car of such ancient vintage that Mio could not guess at its make or nationality. He made no attempt to stop until he reached Mio's car—or perhaps he had been braking for a hundred feet?—but he then came to an instant cessation. Mio waited, in the sudden silence, for the rear of the car to perform an accordion-pleating trick—in the name of simple physics. But nothing happened; Ibáñez and the man at his side were apparently practiced; they didn't even crush their skulls on the windshield. Instead they dismounted and Ibáñez moved toward her as if he were just happening through. To visit the cook, no doubt.

She said pleasantly, "*Buenos días, Señor Ibáñez.*"

"*Ah! La señora! Buenos! Cómo está hoy?*"

"*Muy bien, gracias. Quiere usted tomar café?*"

"No, no coffee, thank you. I don't—I've had—— Do you do this all the days?"

"Take coffee? Or come here?"

"Ah—um."

Mio realized that he was "engaging her in conversation." His associate had meandered with a beautiful nonchalance to her car's side and was examining it as if it were a Jaguar or—even more exotic improbability—a Cadillac. She said, "I usually have a midmorning coffee in my hotel, but at the moment I have no hotel."

Ibáñez showed elaborate surprise.

"No. I am going to Barcelona. But I shall arrive late for coffee. In time for lunch, really." As an afterthought: "The Arycasa has excellent coffee, you know. But this is not bad."

"Good. That is, that it is not bad. Yes, the Hotel Arycasa is one of our best. But I am surprised that you go to Barcelona."

"Are you, señor? You do not recommend Barcelona?"

"Ah, but no! No, I do not not——" He shook his head, as if to clear it, and started again: "I recommend it very much. It is one of our most beautiful cities, a diadem . . ." He pulled up short, abandoned the guidebook, and said, "I had thought that the señora was going to France."

"Ah, now, señor!" Mio regarded her wagging forefinger with astonishment. She had never been coy in her life, and neither had she thought herself much of an actress, but she was certainly throwing herself into this part. She pulled her finger hastily back to join the rest of her and said, "Perhaps you even got the thought from the police form on which I *said* I was going to France?"

"Yes!" Ibáñez registered a slowly dawning recollection— not very well done, but then, Mio thought, not an easy bit to act out. "Yes, you did," he admitted in astounded memory.

She took pity on him. "Well, you know the ways of women. We change our minds. I started northward, but the morning was lovely and I suddenly decided I could not leave your so-beautiful Spain." There, she thought; now you will call me a liar.

But Cobham's prediction was right: Ibáñez swallowed it, painfully, perhaps, but he got it down. He examined her slowly, then he opened his little mouth, said "*Verdad? Adiós, señora*," and he took his small person away in his

63

large, high car. Before he started the frightening engine, however, he bowed down at her from the great height of his seat, smiled tightly, and said, *"Hasta la vista, señora!"*

That Mio didn't like.

South of S'Agaró, perhaps one kilometer's distance, is a particularly high promontory. It juts out over the sea, and as usual the narrow road follows it in the characteristically stubborn and thoroughly frightening fashion. On the right the rock goes still higher, and it too juts out, in its case over the road. The rock is adorned with a few clumps of scrubby pines. All this makes for sporting Spanish driving; one could not possibly see around the curved hill in the first place and the strategically placed additional hazards—pines and jut—prolong the suspense. There are rules to the attacks one makes on this curve (which rules apply to the whole road, since the curve is symptomatic of the whole): As one approaches he accelerates and pulls to the wrong side of the road. This gives a fine and dashing sweep, and if he happens to be going southward, a breath-taking view of the glorious sea and occasionally a swim. But it is undeniably wise to approach even a bull with a modicum of caution, and the Costa Brava road is far meaner than the finest Andalusian bull. The small permissible precaution in the case of the Costa Brava road is to increase the noise that is usual to every Spanish driver. On *this* road one attacks his horn a full thirty seconds earlier, leans harder, and—if, of course, his normal habits permit of such a superlative—more frenziedly.

Cobham's plan had not provided for this contingency.

Mio stopped in the exact center of the curve, hugging the cliff so tightly that, although the sun was on the left, she was half in shadow. She attacked her horn with passion while her mind occupied itself unhappily with her choice of position. It would have been much safer, she decided, had she pulled to the left.

Above her Cobham scrambled from behind the insecure haven of three wispy pines. He slid down the rock, skidded around to the far side of the car (because the right-hand door was jammed against the hill), dove onto the floor in the rear, and shouted, "All right! All right! I hear you!"

Mio shifted into gear, her left hand never ceasing its pumping motion on the horn. "Yes," she yelled, "but can he?"

"Who?"

"Don't know and taking no chances. The man around the bend."

"Oh!" Cobham shouted. "A point well taken!" They had rounded the curve and his voice bellied into beautiful silence. He added in a whisper, "What am I shouting about?"

Mio laughed.

"You sound chipper. All went well?"

"Exactly as you predicted. I'm learning."

"That does not make me entirely happy. Besides, I should have borrowed your shoes. My feet are in ribbons."

"It was only two miles."

"My God!" Cobham said with simple fervor. "If I had realized that I'd never have made it. And then those pines! They need processed plant food. I felt naked."

"Too bad. But if you're going to lead such a life . . ."

They drove in silence for several miles, passing only one motorcycle and a sturdy bicyclist en route. No one passed them. At eleven o'clock the sun made molten sapphires of the sea. Mio said, "Lift your head, Jim, and look ahead. It's beautiful."

He groaned but obeyed. "It is," he said.

"What's that below? Blanes?"

He rose slightly from his squatting position so that he could look downward on the village, and then, his nose almost touching Mio's hair, agreed: "Blanes."

"A country of vistas."

"It is that." He was looking at the heavy twist of black hair on Mio's nape. He said abruptly, "Mio, why are *you* running?"

She didn't answer.

"Turnabout is fair play. When you asked *me* that question, *I* answered. . . . You did something once, so you've gone round concealing your name and hiding ever since. Something like that?"

"Not really hiding. Not actually running. Just—moving."

"What was it?"

For a while it seemed she would again not answer, but finally she said, "I got married."

There was a pause. "It doesn't really clarify, you know. Unless—a wrong 'un?"

"No one thought so. They thought he was a catch. He dropped in on Detroit and all the mothers got excited."

"Including yours?"

"I had no mother. And Uncle and Aunt weren't excitable types." She shook her head. "No, no one pushed me into it. I met him at one of the parties that sprang up all over the place the second he arrived. And I liked him. Maybe all the frenzied competition had something to do with it, but I think I just liked him. He was—uncomplicated. He was young, twenty-six. It's true that I was only eighteen, but

66

Charlie seemed even younger than I." She laughed a little, sadly. "As he was, I suppose. He was quite good looking, then, and well mannered, and of course rich. I don't suppose I ignored that fact. I imagine it was in the back of my mind, as a kind of atmosphere, because—added to his very great name—it would all go to make me a princess, a beloved princess. I was eighteen; it was a little girl's dream. Funny thing—although I certainly know now that I didn't love Charlie, I imagine I would have eventually. Or almost anyone who gave me a chance. I'd guess that no eighteen-year-old is ever in love, but I should think lots of the ones who marry fall in love with their husbands. And I was more lonesome than most and I had enormously romantic views on marriage."

"Not a very good prognosis. Not very easy for Charlie."

"Perhaps not. But it didn't matter. Nothing would have, you see."

"No, I don't. What happened then?"

"Then I divorced him."

"Just like that? When?"

"Nine months later."

There was nothing easy about this, Cobham thought. He had a feeling the story had never been told. Her air of self-containment, her still face, her quiet way of speech—it was all inside somewhere. Which was not a good idea. More for her sake than out of curiosity (the tale had the seeds of the commonplace, he thought) he decided to push on. But he would have to handle it carefully; she would skitter away at a heavy touch.

He backtracked as if what was ahead didn't interest him very much. "Must have given the mothers a nasty turn when you took him off."

"Yes. Little Hermione Heldon. Such a drab child."

"Bet you weren't."

"Nice of you, but I think I was, rather. I was terribly shy, because of the lonesomeness, probably. And Uncle and Aunt meant well but they simply weren't demonstrative. They were old and they had the old idea that well-brought-up children should be absolutely free of conceit, so I had come to believe I was quite ugly. That didn't make me seem any prettier, of course."

"Why an uncle and aunt?"

"They weren't. Aunt was my first cousin twice-removed. My parents died when I was five. An—accident."

Cobham's voice was oddly expressionless. "Too bad," he said.

"My mother got caught behind the wheel of a blazing car. The coroner said that anyone could see that there was no possible hope of removing her alive, but that hadn't kept my father from trying. As a result he died more slowly; took him two nasty days to make his escape. I think Uncle and Aunt disapproved of his—foolishness. I worshiped both their memories.

"The mothers," Mio said after a minute, seemingly out of context and with a smile in her voice. "What made them maddest was that Charlie was an orphan too. Funny, because they had always pitied me, in an annoying, patronizing way, for being in the same state. But with Charlie—well, all the money was his, you see. No waiting for anyone to die, and no in-laws to complicate their daughters' lives."

"You divorced him," Cobham prodded gently.

"Yes." Cobham decided that while her smile was charming, and her real laughter enchanting—the more so for being so unexpected—he didn't like the small laugh at all. "And," she said through the laugh, "you want to know why."

"Well, it does sound a bit limp, you know."

"I divorced him because he—he was nothing. And if *that* sounds a bit limp, I can't help it. I shouldn't think anyone could describe a vacuum." Cobham thought that an excellent job of description, but it didn't make for very high tragedy. So the man was a moron. So what? as they had said in a place he had once visited for a prolonged period. "I got money," Mio said. "It would never have occurred to me, but Charlie's lawyers insisted. They gave me a flat settlement, instead of periodic alimony. I suppose, in view of Charlie's quantities of money, it wasn't a great deal, but it seemed magnificent to me. And, as a matter of fact, it has always been more than enough." She stopped.

Cobham looked at the nape of her neck and thought all this couldn't have happened too long a time ago. The nape was young, and oddly tender. He said, "Mio, my dear, do go on. What happened then?"

"Then? Then I had quite a happy time. I stayed in New York, where Charlie had taken me, and I lived in apartments with other girls. I took one or two jobs because they were fun. I went to parties, all sorts of parties, mostly cocktail parties that lasted until 2 A.M. in the insane American way. I enjoyed everything."

There was a note in her voice . . . Cobham relaxed. He let go his breath, which he hadn't realized he had been holding; he untwisted his right knee . . . Mio had a storytelling note in her voice.

"I was normal," she said in a tone of discovery. "I also got a little conceited. There were quite a lot of men around." I'll bet, Cobham thought. "But I had become more selective. Not bitter, or anything stupid or unwarranted like that.

69

I had no reason to be, of course. But—selective. It's too bad in a way . . ." Her voice trailed off.

Cobham waited.

"That first year," Mio said conversationally, "Charlie remarried twice. The first girl was—well, not unlike me. You know, young and—and respectable. Except she was blond. I remember I read about it and felt sorry for her. Then he picked a widow. She was older than he and she had a—peculiar reputation. That didn't last long either. Next he married a chorus girl off the Copa line. Her picture was all over the papers. She was pretty, if a little frizzy. A blonde. She lasted two months, but she outdid her successor, a platinum-haired, fat, not young burlesque queen. Charlie traveled to Newark to capture *her*. *She* made the run in two days and three nights."

"My God!" Cobham said without volition. "Charles Morningside!"

"Yes." Her voice was flat. "I am one of the Mrs. Charles Morningsides."

"But—the first."

"Does that make it better?" Her voice held a note of true curiosity.

"Better? It's a complete explanation!"

"An explanation?" She shook her head. "It's an apology. I've never bothered to give it."

"You mean you've never tarried long enough to be able to give it."

"That's right. I've never waited around to apologize."

Cobham could think of nothing to say.

The car moved jarringly to the left and Mio let loose another insane cacophony; apparently they were on the approach to a bend. They inclined far to the left, then right, and then settled back as they again reached the straight. The noise stopped and Mio said, "Might as well finish it." Her voice was toneless, dead. "Three years and two months after my divorce, when I was twenty-two, when Charlie had just been divorced by his fifth wife, little hints of what was ahead began to show up. The first time was at a party. The woman was quite drunk, but vertical. She probably didn't realize what she said, and didn't remember it in the morning. I did. When she was introduced to me, she said, 'A wife of Charlie Morningside's? And not a blonde?' . . . Not too crushing, is it? But notice that I had become one of a class, a not too select class. And that was just the beginning. . . ."

The next year Morningside had slowed down. He married only once that year, his sixth wife, but because the pattern had jelled and he had become delightfully newsworthy, his sixth marriage got more notice than the first five put together. The woman was, as were all those to follow, blond, brassy, fat through the middle. She was dressed in a black outfit that was literally open to the waist and was held hesitantly together with laced ties, shod in clubfooted affairs that boasted five-inch heels, soles an inch thick, and thongs that went around and around the ankle and ended in a splash of black satin bows. She showed up in court—after spending twice as much time in the corridors being photographed—and demanded a million dollars for the thirty-six hours of marriage she had endured. She got a part of it, out of court. She also got forty-eight hours of publicity and two night-club engagements, one in the Bronx. "I had her whole —personality—wished on me in the movies," Mio added bitterly, "under the heading of 'News.'"

Cobham was thankful that he couldn't see her face. To picture it without its calmness, its serenity, was very disturbing. It was indecent to remember as much as all this about Morningside's wives. But his idea had been to get it out of her, and out it was coming, a bitter, poisonous stuff, tinctured with bile.

When Mio spoke again, her voice had lost most of the bitterness and had reverted to tonelessness. "So," she said, "I moved on."

"Where?"

"Around the country. Big towns. Then little towns. Then Mexico. Someone always found out. I suppose that when I showed up like that, so suddenly, so aimlessly, it naturally raised questions."

"If it bothers you so much why don't you simply change your name? Legally?"

"My lawyer suggested that. I think it's a silly idea. You have to petition a court. Newspapers would find out. Bigger field day than ever, a sort of new variation on the old theme of Charlie's marriages. And the new name would then become as infamous as Charlie's. Anyway, people would find out. Or, if I became close to them, I'd have to tell them or— or move on."

True enough. Cobham sat silently on the floor.

"It's not a hopeless tragedy; I'm aware of that." Her voice was conversational again. "But if you'll forgive some personal whitewashing, I can make a mildly convincing case out for myself. I was—shy—to begin with. I didn't have a very encouraging childhood. Not what you'd call outgoing. This—this foolishness of caring about being Mrs. Morningside is just a deepening of the original weakness. But . . ."

Her voice trailed off, and then suddenly, passionately, as if it were beyond her ability to shut off the words, as if they had been dammed up for a long time and could no longer be contained, suddenly she spoke again:

"Think," she said, her voice alive, vibrantly pleading; "don't judge without thinking. There's more to my reactions, my fear, my panicky flight than you can see right off. If you're a Mrs. Charles Morningside you're everything that's cheap and opportunist and shoddy. A—a strip-tease girl does something for her money; a Mrs. Morningside needed only to spend a few hours being chased by a fat, fatuous, balding sot—Charlie was old and fat at thirty. She needed only to appear in a courtroom, showing a lot of herself, and she could be sure to get hundreds of times the money the strip-teaser could earn in a lifetime."

"Yes," Cobham said, "I do see, Mio. I do truly see." And because he did, he could think of nothing else to say.

"A Mrs. Morningside," she said flatly, "is a particularly low specimen of prostitute-by-marriage."

. . . Nothing to say.

A few miles farther on Cobham sat up. "We're on the flat," he commented. "Getting into Barcelona, aren't we?"

"Yes. We've hit the ugly stretch."

"Well, then, stop a bit, please." When she drew up to the side of the road, he crawled stiffly out of the back, threw his hat on the floor, and climbed in beside Mio. "Okay," he said, and she moved the car forward. "It's safer for me in front, now," he explained. "In the city's streets I could be peered down upon by pedestrians. And Barcelona is a big city; if we don't run into a particularly well informed bobby I don't think anyone will notice me particularly. Besides, we aren't going far into town."

Mio lifted her eyebrows in inquiry. Her face looked just

the same, he noted with relief. He said, "We stay down here near the waterfront. That way we can get very near the heart of town without really getting up into it. At the Puerto de la Paz—you know it? Where Columbus landed in 1493—as every Barcelonan tells you instantly and inaccurately? Where the tall statue of him is?" She nodded. "Well, just before we get there, I'll get out."

"And then?"

"The rest is up to me, ducks. On my own from there on out."

"But what will you do?"

"Simple and easy. Just a little way up the Ramblas there's a chap. I can get in by the back door—shan't have to walk more than fifty yards. He'll go to still another chap, and get me the means to shed this fancy dress. He'll also get me a ticket for the 9 P.M. boat to Palma. Once in Majorca there are others who'll put me up and find Tony for me. Very simple. Now, about you—you have yourself a nice lunch, and then turn right round and get out of here. Go to the Parellada and eat in high style, why don't you?"

"I could lunch at The Seven Doors. It's right there near the waterfront just before the Ramblas, almost where I'll be letting you out."

"Las Siete Puertas. Capital idea. Good food. Then you turn round and head straight back."

Mio was silent for a few minutes. Then she said, "No. Ibáñez will have telephoned the police to watch for my arrival at the Arycasa, don't you think? So what's the use of making him even more suspicious. I'll go to the Arycasa, check in, and stay a day or so. Then I'll go to France by the Vich road."

"But, my God, Mio! That route crosses the Pyrenees!"

74

"And very beautiful, I'm told." She turned momentarily from the road to smile serenely at him.

"Mio." Suddenly, inexplicably, memory caught up with him. "Morningside died."

She nodded. "Four months ago."

"But that—doesn't that . . ."

"Make it better? No. It'll be some time before his record—there were nine altogether, you know, and he was only thirty-seven when he died—so it'll be some time before his record is matched or forgotten. Probably not in my lifetime."

"I don't remember—what did he die of?"

"Not of paresis and not of cirrhosis of the liver." Unexpectedly her voice broke. "The way he died—hurt me. It's foolish of me, but . . . Charlie died trying to pull his ninth wife out of his burning plane. The papers pointed out that he was drunk as usual or else might not have made the attempt. Apparently it was an impossibility—foolhardy. They hinted, without much veiling, that the concern of his drunken mind might have been his flying license, which the Civil Aeronautics Authority had constantly threatened to take away from him. It—it upset me.

"Then"—her voice hardened—"he meant well, probably, Charlie always meant well—he gave me one last rather sweet slap in the face. Charlie left me his money, all his money, all his thirteen-million-dollars-plus-after-taxes. And if that certainty of publicity wasn't enough, some distant cousins of his immediately announced that they were going to contest the will. They said he was of unsound mind—which, incidentally, is not true; he just didn't have any mind—and they said the first Mrs. Morningside had no right to the money because she had been"—Mio turned to Charlie and

75

smiled—"she had been 'superseded.' I was in Boston, and my lawyer came dashing up there. I said to let them have the money and then Mr. Forster and I had a long wrangle. He won, because he explained that their claim was so baseless that letting them have it would be like giving it to them, and that would make more publicity than anything else I could do. So I said all right and just left it to him and got out of the country as fast as I could because it wasn't going to take long for the reporters to find me. I left the next morning for Gibraltar."

"I see." Cobham paused. Then he said, "That, ducks, is a lot of money to suffer self-pity over. . . . You veer left up here."

Mio veered left. Then she said in a controlled voice, "Self-pity?"

"Why, yes. You suggested that you realized that."

"I realized the possibility, but—not altogether."

"Well, it isn't *altogether* self-pity. Some of it is. Pull up here, please. Just behind the lorry."

When the car stopped, Cobham already had his hand on the door handle. He said abruptly, "This is not a neighborhood for me to hang about in. So I'll go. No point in saying thank you, either. Not expressive enough. Just—*hasta* and God bless." He got out and closed the door. Then he bent and stuck his head back in. "And Mio . . ."

"Yes?" Her face looked very small, very pale, very self-contained.

"Nothing. Good-by."

"Good luck," she called after him. "Good luck, Jim." He turned the corner.

VI

MIO DROVE UP THE RAMBLAS AND ANGLED THROUGH one-way streets to the Arycasa. She registered and was assigned to the same pleasant room she had vacated a few days earlier. (There was an impressively widespread attitude that Barcelona, in its position as metropolis, did not have a "season"—no more than would, for instance, New York or London. Which attitude did nothing to conceal the fact that the Arycasa and all other Barcelona hotels were almost empty in the wintertime.) In her room she did a sketchy bit of unpacking, bathed, and, after lunching at a table overlooking the court, tried for a brief siesta.

She did not sleep. Through her mind, in repetitive succession, filed Cobham—"Cobham the Great"; Davis, with his quiet, withdrawn ways . . . That thought was interrupted by the realization that she had broken her promise to Davis to take him to France. Well, her daybreak flight had been one of panic, not conducive to remembering strangers. And as it turned out it was just as well, since she was farther from France than he. She thought of Westerland's engaging manner and his odd insistence in the discussion of the Astra theft. The palely venomous face of Arthur Jones came uncomfortably to her mind, and was quickly dismissed. The contained fury of Ibáñez evoked a half-smile. The acceptance of the fact that someone had tried to run her off the road was faced and put abruptly aside for a future time. It was the unbidden word—"self-pity"—that absorbed most of the abortive hour. She dismissed it finally with the realization that the degree to which it applied to her mattered not at all. She was what inheritance, events, and personality had made her. Her fears were real and restricting, and even if their basis was merely in her own mind, the situation itself remained unchanged.

She gave up the idea of sleep, dressed, and went down to the lobby.

The clerk said, "It's nice to have you back, señora. And so soon. You found the Costa Brava cold?"

"Yes, a little. Not a good time of year, at any rate."

"One must go in the spring."

"Perhaps I shall," Mio said, knowing she would never again go near that coast. She put her key on the desk and started to turn away, but the clerk said, "A minute, please, señora."

"Yes?" Then she saw the envelope in his hand.

Surprise was delayed for a second; she had taken the envelope and was looking at her name on its surface, written in an ultrafeminine, spidery script, before the realization came that no one knew, no one who would write her could know she was there. The envelope bore no stamp, and that was explained by the underscored instruction in the upper left corner: "A *mano*."

"Something is wrong, señora?"

She looked to her right and, there (how odd to deal with a man at eye level—eye level being only five feet three inches off the floor) was Ibáñez. Mio's face lost its slight smile, and what was left behind was nothing—blankness. Then, the impulse to run having been conquered, she resumed the smile. "*Buenos días, señor.* I'm just your little magnet, aren't I?"

"I beg your pardon?"

"You should have ridden with me."

"It would have been faster," Ibáñez agreed. Was the suggestion that she had been racing, running, fleeing? Or was it merely a comment on the superior speed of her car? "But I did not know then that I would be coming here." A suggestion that he followed where she led? He waited, and when she said nothing, added, "On business." Mio's smile remained present, small and polite; she let no touch of inquiry enter it, so his further explanation became entirely gratuitous: "In search of the thief, the Englishman, the Señor Cobham."

Mio said with mean surprise, "You haven't caught him yet? One man alone, on foot, and so unlike a Spaniard . . . ? My goodness!"

"On foot?"

"I assumed so. Perhaps incorrectly? He had a car?"

"He did not *own* a car."

"Well, then. On foot." Through her blandness she realized that the desk clerk was listening with undue attention; his head swiveled with each of their comments as if he were watching a Ping-pong game. Why the interest? She remembered the letter in her hand.

In the Arycasa, for the past months, Mio's mail had been persistently sent to her room although she had told the mail clerk that sending it up was unnecessary. Mail did not interest Mio. It contained bank statements, advertisements, notes from her lawyer, and, forwarded by her lawyer, a few totally unpertinent letters that acquaintances addressed to her. Getting out of a bed, a bathtub, or a book to accept them seemed thoroughly unnecessary. But the bellboys starved in winter, and so she had not tried too hard to discourage the practice.

But this letter, sent by hand and therefore possibly urgent, had been held at the desk. She had a sudden conviction that Ibáñez had read it, that the clerk knew that (of course), that they were both waiting for her to join them in knowledge of its contents.

She said, indicating the letter, "You will excuse me, señor?"

"Of course." He backed a polite half step.

The flap showed no sign of having been tampered with. She tore it casually, as if the thought of tampering had not occurred to her. The spidery hand was easy to read:

Dear, *dear* Mrs. Heldon,

So delighted you are in town. *Do* hope you can join me for a spot of tea. *Dying* to see you, and may do just that if I can't. As the Spanish say—all the archways of my house are flung open, awaiting your arrival. And if they don't say it quite that way, I'm *sure* you'll *know* what I mean.

Do come, and I'm sorry not to be in a position to ask you to bring friends, but the plants need plant food and we simply can't show the garden; indeed, it shows *us* up. So come alone, for now is the time for all good men & women of Walachia, etc.

Your
S. Drake

P.S. It's #7, you know.

She looked up suddenly and caught the expression of furious impatience and galling impotence on Ibáñez's usually impassive face. She dropped her eyes hastily, to give him and herself a chance to compose themselves. *Her* impulse was to laughter. Poor man. He probably was entirely certain of the writer's identity, but what could he do about it? The answer came, and drove away all amusement: he could follow her. She read the letter quickly through once again, crumpled it casually, and put it on the desk, feeling that the implied unconcern was probably sheer wasted effort. "Well," she said. "It's a nice afternoon. I'm going for a drive. Good day, señor."

He bowed. "Perhaps we will meet again, señora. *Hasta la vista.*"

She walked slowly toward the revolving door. "Again"? More likely that he would never lose sight of her. On the step outside the hotel she smiled vaguely at the doorman, shook her head to his offer of a taxi, and strolled around the corner to her car. Then she sat behind the wheel and stared blankly ahead. Where she should go was transparently clear; to her—not, obviously, to Ibáñez, or he would be there now. But how she should go was less simple. Losing a follower was not a matter in which she had experience. And Cobham should have known that. . . . The fact that he very possibly did know just that, that he was taking a terrible chance that she would not be successful in eluding followers, struck her suddenly and sickeningly. He must be in fairly bad straits to take such a chance. If only it weren't Spain, she thought desperately. In Philadelphia one could go into Wanamaker's; in Detroit there was Hudson's; in Los Angeles, The May Company; in New York, Macy's . . . And in Barcelona there was the Almacenes Jorba, an enormous store, full of cheap merchandise, and—she looked at her watch, five o'clock—crowded at this post-siesta hour. And it was on Puerta del Angel, not far from the waterfront.

She put the car in gear, went slowly through the maze of signals in the Plaza Urquinaona, and turned left into the Vía Layetana.

Cobham was lounging at a table in the rear of Las Siete Puertas, surrounded by newspapers, fronted by a cooler out of which stuck the neck of a green bottle, sipping casually out of a champagne glass—and dressed to kill. Since it was only six-thirty, he had the restaurant to himself; diners would start straggling in at eight, reach maximum at ten-thirty or eleven. The management was thriftily saving its illumination, so the room was lit only by the gray remains of daylight seeping sluggishly through its seven enormous glass doors, and the resultant murkiness gave Cobham the look of a man lounging lazily in his study, too peaceful and too indolent to banish the dusk.

He glanced up and then got up, and said, happily but without surprise, "Hallo! Been shopping?" He came from behind the table to help Mio, who was almost hidden behind a mountain of parcels. They weren't heavy—she had purposely bought objects of little weight—but the effect was imposing. He helped her deposit them on the banquette behind his table, then gazed shrewdly at the pile, and said, "Shopping, hm? You learn quickly, ducks. Was it fun?"

Mio felt a quick surge of anger. She said stiffly, "It was *not* fun. Is this a game, Jim? I got all upset and terribly worried about you and I went through that rigmarole"—she nodded at the parcels—"and was it all for nothing?"

"Nothing? Well, now, that depends on how much one values me. You'll have to answer your own question, I'm afraid, but don't answer hastily. In fact, don't answer aloud. Have some champagne?" He poured some of the too dark wine into a waiting glass. "Spanish, I'm sorry to advise you. Sticky like zabaglione. But it has a pleasantly reminiscent quality. . . . So they were watching you, huh? How did you know?"

"I had no difficulty recognizing Ibáñez," she said dryly, "—not at two paces."

"Ah? Rushed down after us, did he? Now, I don't think showing himself was very smart. Maybe you wouldn't have, ah—gone shopping—if you hadn't seen him."

"Of course I would have. And since he had read the letter, he knew it. That letter scared me. You said—you said you would die."

"It's a possibility, ducks. Not much more. But I thought the letter was an artistic achievement. How did you like the handwriting?"

Mio stared at him with patent annoyance.

"Didn't like it?" He looked saddened. "Now, that's a pity. Poor Great-aunt Sarah!"

"What in the name of heaven have your relatives to do with it?"

"It was Great-aunt Sarah's handwriting. I remembered

those spidery bits I used to receive at school—extremely memorable because they often contained nice spidery checks —and decided that nothing in the world could be more old-maidish."

"Well, you spoiled the effect by mixing your idiom, as usual. Old-maid aunts take tea, but they don't take 'a spot of tea.'"

"Oh dear. Quite right. Afraid I was thinking in terms of scotch."

"Obviously. And, 'all the archways of my house are flung open'—how does one fling open an archway?"

"Ah, but that was the canny dram of Scotch in me. Couldn't very well say 'doors,' could I? A bit close to the mark as it was, but I counted on the fact that Ibáñez could hardly know of our preference for The Seven Doors."

Mio sought a note that would defeat his lightness. "Isn't it dangerous here, Jim?" she asked. Life was real and death seemed earnest and possibly imminent. He ought to be made to acknowledge it. "Or aren't you known here?"

"Indeed I am known. I am a favored patron. But known mainly to Bobby, who has the normal Spanish sense of independence. No mere bobby is going to get a thing out of Bobby. Besides, Bobby is rather fond of me."

"I can imagine. I know Bobby too."

"Bet he's fond of you." He smiled at her, looking like a beneficent faun. "So all is well until about eight. Then, when people start coming, I've got to get out. That poses a pretty problem. But I've got over an hour before I need stare at it, so let's enjoy the hour. Tell me about the chase. I love chases."

"That's probably just as well." She stared irritatedly at his face, which was wreathed in smiling anticipation, laugh lines creasing the roundness at the sides of his eyes, good-natured heedlessness written all over the pink. "You lied to me in the grove," she said suddenly.

"I often lie, ducks. When it seems like good clean fun. What particular lie did I tell you?"

"You said you were afraid, like me."

"Ah, no. We can't have you misquoting Cobham the Great." The lines smoothed out and he became momentarily expressionless. "I said I was like you in that I was afraid. But not 'afraid like you.' Difference, you know."

She stared silently at him, seeing the difference, wishing she could see beyond it.

"Tell me, my pigeon, about how you got here."

"I went shopping," she said absently. "There were two men following me. Not Ibáñez. Rather large men. They made all sorts of mistakes . . ."

"Ah, I like that note. Experienced hares often feel a sort of shame for the hounds. Looking into each other's minds really makes them quite alike."

"I don't agree at all. I believe in—in law and order. In——"

"Order and *then* law. That's what I believe in. So they made mistakes, hm? How?"

"Well, they stayed together, and they stayed near me. Of course, the place was terribly crowded. They couldn't help but know that if I got any distance from them it would be easy to lose me. Especially since I am small." She realized she was apologizing for the hounds and spoke more quickly. "Every time I bought anything I said I would take it with me. Then I'd have to get in a long queue in front of the department's cage, wait to pay for it, and wait for it to be wrapped. It was boring, of course, all that waiting, and the two men got bored. That is, when they weren't embarrassed.

Because I kept buying things like panties, and they were the only men in sight—pitifully obvious and out of place. You know how self-consciously *male* Spanish men like to seem? So—so chest-beating?" She looked inquiringly at Cobham and he nodded with delighted appreciation.

Suddenly she knew it *had* been fun. Making those two large strangers ridiculous, maneuvering them, outwitting them, had been absorbing, interesting, a flight of humor instead of her customary hopeless panic. She acknowledged her realization with a reluctant smile, and Cobham's widening grin showed that he understood. She reached across him and picked a parcel at random. She tore it open and found she had hit on one of the best of the lot, the chemise—a nightmare of mauve flounces, shirred lace, tucks, net inserts, and coy bows. She held it up and watched Cobham's eyes widen.

He said with awe, "Oh no, ducks. Oh no!" and went into a paroxysm of laughter.

"Yes," she said complacently. "And I held it up in the store, too. This is only a sample. You should see the panties —they have sequins. That store is a treasure chest. Well, when I came to the eleventh purchase I kept my back to the two men, gave the saleswoman my name and address and told her to send it, that the desk clerk would pay for it. Then I started toward the cashier's cage in the usual way. The two men just watched me—it was routine by then and they were—were sort of dulled, I think. Halfway to the cage I found myself in a convenient mob, so I sort of folded a little to make myself shorter and scuttled off in another direction. I kept going, and fast, until I got to the ground floor. Then I picked an exit on the opposite side from the one I had come in and"—she spread her hands—"here I am. I imagine they wasted a full minute or two, figuring that I'd show up in that queue any second.

"But then I had to carry all the stuff here, because I was afraid that the business of throwing it away would create such a riot that it would draw the *policía*." She watched while he envisioned that possible scene, disapproved of his delight, and decided to dampen it: "You owe me *quinientas*."

"All that for *quinientas*?" He eyed the mound with respect. "You'd make a wonderful wife."

It wasn't the reaction she had expected, but in welcoming the appearance of Bobby she was thinking of more than its diversionary quality; Bobby's English, fluent but almost unbelievable, always delighted her.

Bobby came happily toward her, light glinting off him with the same effect of warmth that a Christmas-tree ornament achieves. His bald pate shone, his smile beamed, his eyes glistened, and the starched white linen sheathing his arms, as he extended them in welcome, threw little rays in her direction. He greeted her in his magnificent Brooklynese, spoken as if by a cabdriver on De Kalb Avenue. Bobby had spent almost fifteen years in the dining room of a hotel on Brooklyn Heights, and his English was unaccented—in the ambiguous sense that a Brooklyn waiter's English is unaccented. Mio had spent many happy evenings in Las Siete Puertas looking down into her wineglass, carefully controlling her facial muscles while bewildered Britishers struggled to find a foothold and sometimes gave up and asked for the French-speaking waiter, preferring the known hazard to the unknown. On a few occasions she had acted as an interpreter—between Bobby and a confused Australian honeymoon couple, a commercial traveler from Liverpool who obviously wished himself back in the rain, and—best of all—the Scotsman who literally had no idea what language Bobby was speaking, and whose English was so far from Mio's that negotiations had bogged to a point at which American Indian smoke signals would have been a clarifying factor.

Bobby was delighted to see her; Bobby would bring more wine, but fast; Bobby thought they should have some oor doover and would take care of it instantly.

"Quite a chap, Roberto. And I was right—he loves you dearly."

"He is a married man, sir."

"Ah, then you have got as far as a discussion of that fact? Hasn't he got a magnificent accent? Can't you just see dirty old Brooklyn Bridge rising above him as he speaks?"

Mio looked at him thoughtfully. "*I* can, but it's surprising that *you* should."

"Oh. I expect it is. Well, ducks, I am a man of parts."

"Huh. Peculiar parts. An Englishman may know New York, Hollywood, Detroit, even Milwaukee or Texas, but he doesn't usually feel nostalgic about the Brooklyn Bridge. I had thought it—odd—for an Englishman to be involved in an American robbery but since you are so knowledgeable about Brooklyn . . ."

Cobham lifted his eyebrows. "American robbery?"

"The Astra affair. Did you think I was unconscious during that whole discussion? It was perfectly obvious that a—a hare-and-hounds business was going on, but until you beat it out like that, I couldn't decide who——"

She stopped because Cobham was drowning her out with shouts of laughter. Between gasps and rockings he kept saying, "Oh no, ducks! Oh no!"

Mio watched him coldly. When he subsided slightly, she asked frigidly, "Oh-no-what?"

"I'm sorry." He tried to stop laughing, but little yelps kept escaping him. "I'm truly sorry. I'm not laughing at you, but at the picture of me in any such million-dollar league. Me and Alec Guinness and the Bank of England. Lovely, dashing thought, Mio, but I'm not your man. I——" He struggled, gave up, and rolled forward in an extravagance of glee. Bobby reappeared, characteristically, irresistibly drawn by the emotion he prized most highly.

Mio's frigid stare sent Bobby fleeing back around the bar, and to a minor degree it sobered Cobham. Her question sobered him a little further. "Didn't you wonder, then, why I asked no questions?"

He simmered to a smile. "I thought you were the woman of my dreams."

"If that's your dream, you might as well wake up. There is no such woman on earth. You said you were a thief, in just so many words. Well, what have you stolen?"

"Ah." The pink face developed an expressionless, lineless roundness. "It isn't quite so simple as all that. I have—appropriated—that which the Spanish Government wishes to get to first."

"Double talk," Mio commented coldly.

"Yes, expect it is. Well, my dear, I run a black market, the best-organized, most businesslike black market in Spain." He looked at her out of the corner of his eye appraisingly, and the peeking gesture surprised her. It was so unlike Cobham to test her, or anyone, for reaction. Or was her assumption that he was above caring for the world's opinion a foolish one? Did everyone care—if not as passionately as she did, at least to some degree?

She said, "That's a very short story, Jim."

"Well, what more is there to say?"

"Start somewhere. For instance, why should you, an Englishman, be involved in a Spanish black market?"

"That's an easy one. Everyone likes to discuss his profession or trade." He smiled at her and her doubt of the minute before was dispelled. Jim was enjoying himself again. "You see, the Spanish Government gives you, or anyone, 39.86 pesetas for your dollar, an Englishman gets 110.94 for his pound. But if you buy pesetas almost anywhere else on earth you get considerably more. For instance, you can get almost two hundred and fifty dollars' worth of pesetas in the States for two hundred dollars. No?"

"Yes."

"Well, the same is true for an Englishman, Frenchman, and so on. So the market is there, the money is to be made, and someone is bound to make it. We simply cater to the market in the manner of time immemorial."

"You haven't answered my question—why an Englishman?"

"Simple enough. After we give you more pesetas for your dollar, franc, pound, or whatever than the *cambios*, or the banks, we must convert that currency, which we obviously cannot do in Spain. An outsider is needed. I am that outsider. And the outsider, in my case and in most cases, usually becomes the—the, uh, guiding force. He is the indispensable member, you see. If he has brains, initiative, foresight"—he let a note of young-man-rising-in-his-profession creep into his voice—"get-up-and-go, he proceeds to head his, uh, organization."

"But you can't dispose of the money in England."

"And how very right you are. But there is Tangiers, Gi-

90

braltar, even a place just over the Pyrenees. Other places."

"I see." She added deliberately, "How very distasteful."

His face froze. "So much worse than a million-dollar thief?"

"No. No, of course not. I——" She stopped.

"Less glamour, perhaps? And yet sums in themselves should mean nothing to a millionairess."

Mio turned on the banquette to face Cobham directly. "I don't know why I'm upset. So particularly upset. I thought you were the Astra thief. I accepted that. I don't know why . . ."

"Perhaps because it was unexpected." His face was still stiff, and the smile he put on it did nothing to warm it. "But you should watch yourself, my dear. If you had been championing the Astra thief you would have been helping a murderer—a quadruple murderer. Had you thought of that? I suppose you had not. *Why* you accepted the role of champion of a thief is pretty clear, my dear. You're identifying yourself, classifying yourself, with the fleer. And it's a bad mistake. I talked you into conveying me to Barcelona because I'm an opportunist. I needed you, and I was willing to enlist your help. But I think badly of myself. Because you are not doomed to flee. You should—— Ah, well." He stood up and said, "Thank you for coming, ducks. Forgive the quality of the champagne and accept my thanks for the drive down, which I seemed unable to offer earlier." He hesitated and then held out his hand, for the shaking.

Mio made no move to take the hand. She stared at him, and then she started to laugh. He stared back in uncharacteristic bewilderment, momentarily out of the driver's seat.

"The outfit," she gasped, pointing at his vest. "The—the —the beautiful——" Her lovely laugh threw cascades of musical sound against the dark walls and instantly brought Bobby back. He peeked happily around the edge of the right-angled bar.

"This?" Cobham fell quickly back into character. "You gaze upon my apparel?" He looked down at his jacket. "Well, the check *is* a bit large, but the red feathers or down or—what do you suppose those tufts *are?*—the red whatever is practically not noticeable. And the trousers are most subdued."

"The vest! That vest!"

"You don't like the color of the sun? Well, it's that or my tummy. Shirt won't close. Can't think what that chap's waistline must measure."

"Perhaps *your* waistline is getting out of hand."

Bobby looked sad at such tactlessness.

"That," Cobham said mournfully, "is a possible but uncharitable solution. This fellow, the collection's earlier possessor, is a sportin' type, don't y'know? Not huntin'-fishin'-sportin'—but I'm sure you follow me."

Mio saw Bobby's face. Bobby was happy, just because everyone else was happy. And he clearly thought Cobham looked superb. "Bobby likes the—the ensemble. Don't you, Bobby?"

"An' how!"

"There. So you can stop showing off and sit down."

Bobby went happily off, the moment passed, and Cobham resumed his seat without a noticeable change of pace. But he said, "Before we tactfully drop the subject, I'd like to say one thing more about my—my business. I would not actually state that mine is an honest endeavor, and I certainly wouldn't pretend that I am an honest man, Mio, but there is just a little something to be said for black-marketeering of

92

this sort. I commented before that I believe in 'order and then law.' If this money business were properly ordered, the laws would make sense. They are not; they do not. It becomes inevitable that they will be flouted."

"And that you must be the flouter? Oh well, drop it—I'm no judge. Let's get down to cases—what's happened? Why did you send for me?"

"Trouble. They're on to me. To all of us. They're cleaning up with a vengeance—an insane vengeance, since another group will go into business immediately. They know it, and they'll do nothing about them for a devil of a time. But— they seem determined to clean *us* up. That means that all the retreats that I could normally hole up in are closed to me. Chaps are scattering. The one whose flat I went to this afternoon took that note up near the Diagonal and paid a kid to deliver it; that was the last favor he could do me. Outside of getting these clothes, which you don't consider a favor."

"Well, they hardly serve to make you inconspicuous," Mio murmured. "Especially the vest."

"Better than appearing as a belly dancer."

"I'm not so sure. What now? You're waiting here until the nine-o'clock boat for Majorca?"

"A forgotten dream, that. That pier, my friends tell me, is alive with police. Crawling. An impossibility."

"They know about your English friend?"

He looked surprised. "Oh no. No chance of that. I wouldn't blacken Tony's name by mentioning it. No one but you and I knows about Tony. But it is traditional for Barcelonans on the run to dash for the Baleares."

"Well, what *can* you do? Walk across the Pyrenees?"

"Wouldn't have a hope. Biggest trouble is I look so confoundedly un-Spanish. And that has given me an——"

She interrupted: "Jim, if they catch you—what? Prison?"

He sat still for a minute. Then he called out, "Bobby! How about a little light to pierce this gloom?" Bobby came running. The lights went on, and Mio had a clearer view of Cobham's smiling face. There was something different about the smile. "Prison?" he murmured contemplatively. "Well, if I'm lucky, ducky."

She stared at him.

"Most unlike them, y'know," he murmured. "Peaceful, law-abiding people, the Spanish. But they seem to be up in arms. Literally. They're popping off popguns very easily these days."

Mio felt cold.

"Now"—Cobham was suddenly all animation—"I started to tell you my idea. The business of my looking so damnably un-Spanish is what gave it to me. Fault of my coloring of course, but mainly my hair, don't you know? So I thought I'd make a rather jolly monk. What do you think?"

"Monk? You've lost me."

"Cling tight, because here we go. I have an acquaintance who was once, briefly, I should imagine, a Benedictine brother. A lay member of some sort, never got ordained. Or whatever. Lucky for the entire order—he's a rascal. However, he still had the soutane and he lent it to me. This afternoon." He gestured, and Mio saw a newspaper-wrapped bundle under the end of the banquette. "It has a lovely cowl."

"And just by putting that thing on you're going to be able to stroll around Barcelona like—like an ostrich?"

"No, no, my dear. Of course I do not intend to stroll about Barcelona. The place to make even a sparkling diamond like myself unnoticeable is among a whole jeweler's tray of diamonds, isn't it?"

She stared at him. "Montserrat," she murmured.

He beamed. "You always surprise me, and so pleasantly, little Mio. The Benedictine monastery is on Montserrat. Exactly."

"Now all you have to do is get there. Thirty miles, about."

"Ex-act-ly!"

"—uphill. And that's where I come in."

"Ex-act-ly!"

"And that's not so easy."

"You interrupt my litany, and most distastefully. Why isn't it easy?"

"At this point, Jim, they're not only looking for you. Ibáñez and cohorts are anxious to see me, too. I betcha, huh?"

"Huh."

"And they certainly haven't forgotten my nice dirty little Citroën, which is still standing lonesomely in front of the Jorba."

"Not so lonesomely," he murmured.

"Ex-act-ly."

"Hm." He pondered, and the pause stretched to a minute's worth. Then he turned, smiled at Mio, and said, "But I am an ingenious fellow. And you tend to inspire me. The comment you made a few minutes ago about bringing your purchases here . . . Two points: On payment of *quinientas pesetas* this stuff"—he indicated the mound of parcels—"is mine, huh?"

"Huh."

He reached into the canary-colored vest, brought out a wallet, and passed over a five-hundred-peseta note. "I am now in honorable possession of this loot, and may do with it as I please.

"Second point: Would you not say that the Spanish are a delightfully childish people, in the nicest sense of the term? Eager, interested in everything, curious in the pleasantest way, happy to be amused . . . ? Lovers of circuses, bull-fights, opera, flamenco, street fights, and anything in the least out of the ordinary . . . ?"

"If you take dead aim, you might just possibly hit the point."

"Ah, curious yourself, are you? Well, now, watch Cobham the Great. . . . Bobby!"

Bobby appeared at his usual trot.

"Bobby, it will be an hour before you have a crowd here. Do you think you could get that hour off?"

"*Ay, no, señor!*" Even in vast regret Bobby retained his smile. "*El patrón——*"

"—for a mil?"

As if he had not been interrupted, Bobby said, "I could sure get a n'our off."

"This will involve you with the police."

"Trouble is, ya see," Bobby said, switching ground without losing even the edge of the smile, "der ain't nobuddy here but me an' da *chico*."

"But you will have done nothing wrong. *Absolutely nothing wrong.* And, omitting to mention my name, you will otherwise tell the exact truth, blaming everything on the Señora Heldon. You will tell them *she* gave you a thousand pesetas, not that I did. You will tell them *she* gave you your instructions, not that I did. This is to keep her out of trouble. Because what she is going to pay you to do, and what you are

96

going to do, is absolutely harmless—if my name is not mentioned. *Claro?*"

"*No, señor. No es claro. Es——*"

"The words 'shill' and 'spiel'—do you understand them?"

"Come straight outta my secon' country."

"I thought so. Well, now, here's what you do . . ."

VII

WITH COBHAM AT HER ELBOW IT HAD ALL SEEMED possible, plausible—even amusing. Away from Cobham it was manifestly ridiculous, childish, sure of failure. She stood inside the Jorba, near the main doors, but out of sight of the street. By peeking diagonally to her left, through the glass door, she could see her car, and beyond it, across the street, the man leaning against the fender of another parked car. She checked her watch. Fourteen minutes to eight. Bobby should have been in action for one full minute now, but the man across the street hadn't moved.

Someone came through the door and sounds of commotion came with him. Mio took a deep breath.

Off to her right she saw a woman enter and speak to two other women. The three rushed outside. The man across the street stood upright.

Mio took a step toward the door.

The man took a few steps down the center of the street.

Three cars stopped in the middle of the street. Apparently there was a jam ahead of them. The man in the street rose on his toes, but he couldn't see over the cars. Then he walked swiftly between two cars, veered past Mio, and went beyond her area of vision.

Mio opened the glass door and stepped out beside the show window.

Through it, a hundred feet down the street to her right, she could see a mob; there were sounds of laughter, and also of an incipient fight. Cobham had said there would be a fight. At least one, he had said.

Above the sounds of the crowd she could hear Bobby's happy voice. He certainly did have a circus barker's voice. Then she saw the policemen. One passed in front of her. Another, wearing the white arm bands of a traffic cop, was moving quickly along the opposite side of the street.

She looked down at her wrist: it was twelve minutes before eight. Cobham had said to start after three minutes. He predicted a seven- to ten-minute upheaval. But one thing he hadn't figured on—the traffic jam.

Mio ran lightly to her left, keys in hand. Key in ignition. Car in gear. And then she stared helplessly at the almost solid block of cars in front of her. Her eyes moved to the rear-view mirror. She was almost at the corner and the parking area behind her was free. She switched to reverse, moved back to the corner, hesitated, realized that there was no room in which to turn, and so, still in reverse, rounded the corner. She climbed the curb, righted herself, and took the whole block in fast reverse. It was a short street, and narrow, and dark. And one way. One way in the direction she was facing but not in the direction she was traveling. Still, all the police in the vicinity seemed to have joined Bobby. She hoped. Thirty seconds later she came out into the Ramblas, rear first, put her car into forward gear, said a prayer of thanksgiving, made a three-quarter turn around the promenade, and drove sedately toward the waterfront.

And as she drove a surprising realization came to her. During the past half hour she had not been afraid. Her pulse had probably beat a little faster, but so had her mind worked a little faster. And she had not been at all frightened.

The exterior of The Seven Doors was as badly lit as ever; she could see nothing. But before she had come to a stop, Cobham appeared from behind one of the big pillars that supported the ancient stone portico. She wondered how he could move so fast and still seem to be idling. He spared a second to grin at her, and then dove into the back of the car. The door slammed and he said, "Cobham has resumed his usual position—flat on his face. Westward ho!"

Mio didn't move. "Lovely thought," she said, "but there is one little thing you didn't include in your plans."

"Yes?"

"The road to Montserrat lies smack on the other side of town. It is true that the streets are lit by gaslight, but it's still an admirable job of lighting. Would you like to sail gloriously through on the Vía Layetana? Or do you prefer the flares, flowers, and fountains of the Ramblas?"

He said hastily, "Neither, for heaven's sake. Stick to the waterfront. Go round the city."

She smiled in the darkness and put the car into gear. At least she had made Jim speak quickly.

When Mio had made a wide circle around Montjuich and the river Llobregat and they had reached the darkness of Route N 11, Jim crawled up onto the back seat and said, "Well! Well, indeed. All is. How did it go?"

"Exactly as scheduled. Beautifully. Except for a small traffic jam. I had to back out. Otherwise . . . Bobby was superb. I only got a glimpse, but it was enough. He must have been standing on something, because he rose over the crowd, and he had apparently given away about half the junk. He was holding up the sequined panties with one hand and with the other he was trying to hold onto the half-dozen packages he had left. And he was in fine voice. Wish I could understand Catalan. Would have loved to hear his explanation."

"I warned him to stay away from any note of 'share the wealth.' A suggestion of communism, and he'd have had it. Were the cops coming?"

"In force."

"Half hour in the police station and they'll turn him loose in disgust. *You'll* be their pigeon, my pigeon. You know what you'll say?"

"I shall explain that it was a whim. I'd had two bottles of champagne, and it was a whim."

"They will call you a liar, politely enough since you are *norteamericana*—but a liar. Incontrovertibly. They will mention me. They will threaten. And you will say . . . ?"

"That it was a whim. Two bottles of champagne. You know *norteamericanas* . . ."

"Good girl. Proud of you. Sorry about all of this."

"All right. But—one odd thing happened. Didn't happen."

"What was that?"

"I wasn't afraid."

"Ah?"

"I thought about it afterward. As I was driving back to pick you up."

"Any conclusions?"

"Just that the reason wasn't—dramatic. You know, scared soldier suffers for several thousand feet of film, and then rushes into the teeth of two hundred men, saves twelve comrades, and is cured for all time."

"Nothing like that?"

"I wasn't afraid because it wasn't for *me*. I wasn't involved, except physically. So—nothing to be afraid of or for."

"I see. And that doesn't suggest a possible solution?"

"You're thinking of the second feature. *Love Thy Neighbor*. Good picture, but moral not applicable. I'm perfectly willing to love my neighbor, but my neighbor sneers. Different story, see?"

He didn't answer.

Mio said, "What's your movie, Jim?"

"How do you mean?"

"What are you afraid of?"

"Oh, that. I'm the character in the first film. I'm afraid of blood."

"Blood?" The surprise was clear in her voice.

"Bad word. Say, violence. What did you expect, my dear? Something deeply psychological? Well, I'm just afraid. Simple as that."

"But this—this business you're in?"

"Bloodless. Normally. It's a financial venture. The current situation is as unusual as—oh, as a man in the City getting run over by a lorry. Not predictable when he chose a City career."

"But the—the chase. Living on the floor of my car. That sort of thing wasn't entirely unpredictable. And you said you enjoyed chases."

"Invigorating," he agreed happily.

"But violent!"

"Oh no. Exciting, pulse-racing. When I say violence, I mean just that. A little more than that—man-made violence. I'm not afraid of illness, I'm not afraid of death. For myself or others. But I want to die in bed. I want my loved ones—say, my sister—to die in bed. I don't want to shoot or be shot at. I don't want to hit or be hit. Very simple. Very powerful fear."

"What happened in the war?"

"My final downfall," he said promptly. "I was a healthy young man of twenty-five in 1939. I had no responsibilities, no illnesses. I couldn't even plead honest pacifism, or moral scruples. I wasn't stupid and so it seemed clear enough that we had to fight. But—not me. The alternative was jail. Didn't sound good to me, so—I skipped. Lost myself. Pretty shocking for my relations, you know. Until then they had covered up my—peculiarity—as much as possible. I was most atypical as an English schoolboy—'Get out there and fight!' and 'The game's the thing!'—that stuff didn't clutch at my breast if it meant shoving someone about, or being shoved. And some of those bloody games are amazingly—bloody. But it was the war that really blew it. And after the war I found myself in quite some disrepute. Drifted into this sort of thing. And, if you'll try not to be shocked, I drifted pretty far. Into an American cooler once."

She *was* shocked. She said nothing.

"The real disgrace was its location. It was a Brooklyn hostelry, called the Raymond Street Jail, and I spent five informative months there."

"So accounting for your being a 'man of parts.'"

"Partially. Also accounting for West's reaction to my idiom. He is apparently pretty well versed in such lingo himself."

"And so this fear of violence accounts for your—your way of life?"

"Not a bit of it. Seeds of this kind of life are deep in me. I like it. Enjoy it. Don't want anything else."

Mio's dark head was motionless.

"Tell you something else," Cobham said slowly. "Like you, I've never told anyone This, My Story. Unlike yours, though, it's not unknown. Quite a number of people remember it, or the name. Doesn't bother me unduly. Not nice, of course, but inevitable."

"What are you talking about, Jim?"

"Oh, got rather off the point, didn't I? Because I'm embarrassed, I suspect. Not by the story itself. That's just a plain tragedy, and sordid. But because a psychiatrist—I'm wandering again, huh? Well, my father killed my mother. With a knife. Very messy. Tried to kill himself. Wasn't so successful. Was hanged. Much newspaper space. When you told me you were orphaned at five and by violence, it occurred to me that fellow-Walachians probably often have similar heritages, similar fears, similar fates. You were five; I was six. Coincidence, huh? And we're both—marred. Not such a coincidence. But—the embarrassment I was talking about. The psychiatric angle. Imagine I'd be a psychiatrist's nightmare. So clear—so unsubtle—so unburied. I saw blood and violence; I don't like blood and violence. Straightforward, huh? But my sister saw it too; she was eight. And she hasn't any such quirk. *She* got well into the war and did her bloody bit. But—she has been married four times. Much more interesting for a psychiatrist, huh?"

"Huh," Mio said. It was a sad little syllable.

"But I'm sure there's no cause and effect between my fear of violence and what I like to think of as my Robin

Hood complex. Robin Hood makes it all sound charming, doesn't it?"

"Robin Hood," Mio said thoughtfully. "Was it a Robin Hood complex that brought you to S'Agaró? In February?"

There was a moment's quiet. Then Cobham said, with an effect of carefulness, "How do you mean? I don't follow you."

"Why not? Straight question."

"Yes, it is that." Then he laughed. "Mio, little Mio. Full of surprises. Yes, to your question. Yes, it was the Robin Hood complex."

Mio said nothing.

"But maybe not altogether."

Mio still said nothing.

"Are you tantalizing me with silence, ducks?" He paused. "If so, it's working. Robin Hood stole from the rich to give to the poor, didn't he? And best of all he liked to steal ill-gotten gains, no?"

"The Astra money. Had you chosen your charity yet, Jim?"

"No. . . . There it is, ahead. See Montserrat? No, I had not chosen my charity. Tell me, Mio, how do you do this?"

"Do what?"

"Ask the right question, make the exact response. All of a sudden. Without knowledge. I think, without knowledge."

Mio's head swiveled in the dimness.

"No, I think you don't know. I think you didn't figure out that I shouldn't be there—in February—when no one was there—without a reason. That the reason was the money. All that money. Streaming in. Suddenly the Costa Brava—S'Agaró, and the rest of it, and Barcelona itself—became the font of dollars. I certainly never dreamed of the

Astra money. But there *was* money, money in quantities, and I knew it wasn't honest money. Honest money doesn't get cashed in like that. Not in quantities, in dollars, on the black market, out of season. If you have that kind of money, your bank does it for you; and not out of season; and you're well known, everyone is aware of your presence. So I—I went to see."

"You thought you might as well get the money at the source."

"Now you're an eighth of a step ahead of me. That thought had flickered very briefly through my mind. But mainly I was curious. And I wondered what the others would do."

"Others?"

"Black markets are complicated organizations. I am never alone. That which I could see the outlines of in Paris, where I happened to be, must have been even clearer here. And of course it was. That's why I'm now running, I suspect. Jaime."

"Jaime." The name meant nothing, and then Mio said, "The *bartender*?"

"My dear, the head bartender, especially if he's a linguist, in the big hotel in any tourist town in a country of debased currency is an important factor in the local black market. As I see it, Jaime was coming round to my conclusions. He was being a bit slow about it, but then the sight of me consolidated all his suspicions. He's not supposed to know me, but there's no doubt that, faced with my nationality, physical description, mannerisms, he put it all together. If the *jefe* was interested, he had been right all along. The *jefe* wouldn't be there unless . . . So he decided to get rid of me and he called in Ibáñez."

"But what about Jaime himself? He was implicated. Wasn't—didn't . . . ? I don't understand."

"Very simple. He didn't think. Having blabbed, he was stopped. Then he—— Well, you people call it 'turning state's evidence,' and a lovely phrase it is. He'll get nothing out of it, for good or bad, but he didn't think that quite through. All this accounts for the present avidity of the police. They've got a chance to clean everything up beautifully, you see. With a pat of approval from the Generalísimo himself. Because Jaime can say so much. Then he'll tend bar as usual and next May he'll tie up with the next contingent of black marketeers. It's no real loss to Jaime, but for one silly moment he thought it was going to be a big gain. He would first get rid of me and then see what he could do about getting hold of all that nice money floating around the coast."

"And when did Astra get into it?"

"Why, when I arrived in all my innocence, and found two charming American gentlemen who seemed to discuss nothing but the Astra robbery."

"So?"

"So I joined in the discussion. 'Egged them on,' as one says in Brooklyn. What else was there to do? I had to know who was chasing whom, and how things stood. Never did find out. Not conclusively."

"Strange mountain, Montserrat." Mio tilted her head at the towering, rugged thrust in front of them, rising dark and gaunt from the plain.

"*Mons-serrat*, saw-toothed mountain. A part of the whole. Have you never toured the north of Spain?"

"No."

"Drive, sometime, from Barcelona to Salamanca. Through

the heart, through Zaragoza and Madrid. You ride for barren miles, on a single barren road, through a barren land. Nothing grows, although near Ávila you have the illusion that rocks are growing. Magnificent rock formations, mile after barren mile. And while you ride that road, the only road, a straight road, with never a fruit or vegetable or vineyard to break the bleakness, you have the prospect of glory, because great, tall, distant mountains, gaunt and snow-capped, ride in an unbroken chain beside you, and stand ahead of you in threatening promise. The odd thing is that, surrounded by mountains as you are, even if they are vastly distant, you should feel that you are in a valley—caged, depressed—but instead you have the sense of being on a plateau, riding to land's end; of being on top of a world off of which you will eventually fall. You *do* have a sense of mental depression, but it is caused by the isolation, by the utter desertion and lack of life; not by any realization that you are caught in a bowl, the sides of which are formed by monstrous giants. But Montserrat"—he nodded toward it in the darkness, although Mio could not see him—"Montserrat contradicts all this because one *does* arrive at Montserrat. One climbs its four thousand feet and so proves it fallible and destroys the illusion of an infinity."

"That was a very male speech," Mio said dryly. "Women rarely permit themselves illusions of inaccessibility, impenetrability, infinity. Things *are* impossible to us, or they're not. And the reason you do it is excessively male. If you can talk yourself into the idea that something is practically impossible, and then succeed in overcoming it—why, then you can say you've done the almost impossible. See?"

"Um. And women are excessively clever at trying to reduce us and our accomplishments to the level of small boys. What about your conviction that it is impossible for anyone to accept you for what you are without coating you with the motives of your successors-in-marriage? Did you erect that as a challenge to yourself, or to males, or——"

"*Now* you're being feminine. Using attack as a defense. Your wife must have had a trying time."

"*Wife?*" Cobham's voice rose a full octave, and cracked. "I never had a wife!"

"You *said* you did!"

"Did I? Ah yes, the widower remark. It was a lie."

She turned to fix him with a second's stare, and then looked back at the dark road. "Just like that."

"But that's the best kind of lie, my dear. There are only two possible kinds of lies—the necessary, and the aimless. Necessary lies, well, you save your neck. Not pretty, but one does now and then. The other kind brightens the moment. It was much prettier to say I was a widower, because it was perfectly clear that those two were bachelors, and then I had the next comment, you see?"

"No."

"You know, I suspect you do, I really suspect you do, although I was just asking idly, and I have no intention of making you admit it. But you just may have the ability to brighten the day. . . . Ah well, I have certainly never married. Certainly not!"

"Wouldn't that brighten the day? Brighten just the one, maybe?"

His voice held a smile, but he said, "No, it would shadow the day with horror."

" 'Horror' seems a strong word," Mio murmured.

"Well, perhaps the key word was 'shadow,' y'know. Just think—just *think*—what I, or any man, promises in a wedding ceremony. 'Here and now I promise to renounce about half the fun, two thirds of the joy, and one quarter of the adventure in the world. I am saying, I am promising, I am trying to mean and believe that never again will I look at a pretty face with fixed intention to do or die. I am giving up several hundred women and the possibilities in several million. The little types who plead with you with their eyes to believe that they are delicate and breakable, and who tell you with every other inch of them that they are made of pliable tissue, made to be plied. The big ones, who seem to say, "I know I'm too much of a challenge for you." The ones who look haughty, the ones who look humble. The ones who refuse to look at you at all. The ones who know—and the ones who don't.'" He laughed. "No," he said, "I've never married."

"Well, then, lucky woman."

"Now, now, ducks. I want it both ways. Lucky me, unlucky woman. Huh?"

"Huh." The road had become a slight ascent. "Do we have to climb all four thousand feet of this challenge?" she asked.

"I'm hungry. . . . No. The monastery is cuddled cozily into a sort of nook in the mountain. A little less than two-thirds' way up. We seem to have got off the subject. I was accusing you of creating a challenge because you're afraid——"

"Want to try to find something to eat in one of these little villages?"

"Good heavens, no! At this hour, on this road, we would be notable and reportable curiosities. I shall have to starve."

"Then maybe you'll fit into that vest."

"You remind me, ducks, that I must effect my change of

personality. I shall become pious and kindly—and jolly. For what is jollier than a jolly fat monk?"

The car took a turn, left the flat, insipid countryside, and started abruptly skyward. After ten minutes of steady climbing in the darkness—a darkness now deepened by the road's wooded perimeters—Mio's headlights picked out a sign: "Monestir—," it said, "Monasterio—Monastère—Kloster—Monastery."

"Ah!" Jim said with complacence. "I shall suit this order. I too believe in clarity, brevity, and a touch of self-advertisement."

Minutes later the road flattened out, and at Cobham's instruction Mio stopped the car. She was on the edge of a large and, at that hour, empty car park that took up almost all the flat surface of the "nook" that was not covered by the monastery itself and its accompanying buildings. A sprinkling of lights flickered in the monastery and in the little community that huddled at its heels. But the lights were outshone by the stars, and the buildings were overwhelmed by the wild, improbable, frightening immensity of the towering pinnacles. The sheer, ragged precipices that rose behind the seventeenth-century masonry dated themselves not in centuries but in millenniums, and by their awesome majesty belittled the size and beauty of the man-made structures.

It was very still. Mio said, "I feel small."

"You *are* small, ducks. But I know what you mean." He opened the door, got out, and stood beside Mio, gazing upward with her at the dark, stark, perpendicular slabs of stone that so dwarfed him and her. "I feel small myself."

Mio looked out at the monkish figure beside her and

smiled. The flowing robe added a dozen pounds to Cobham's appearance. But he *did* look jolly. "You are not small, Jim; let me reassure you on that point. And you entirely destroy the sense of magnificence that had come over me."

"My own magnificence belittles it?"

"That was not *exactly* my thought."

"You will regard my dignity with respect, señora."

"*Sí, señor.* Or do I say, Brother . . . ?" Her voice changed. "Jim, I am worried about you. Am I supposed to drive off and just—just leave you here?"

"That's it, ducks."

"But what will you do?"

"I'm simply full of ideas. I shall nip into one of those buildings and sleep. Perhaps the *explanada* there." He nodded at the porticoed pavilion above them. "I shall join a soup-kitchen line. I shall lose myself in scholarly research in the library stacks. The followers of St. Benedict are most scholarly and literary. Or maybe I'll assault that little Everest there, and contemplate my navel."

"The Benedictine Brother role is sufficiently unconvincing—please don't add to it by confusing yourself with Tensing. *Or* with Buddha. And what about your Spanish? It isn't the best."

"I can always manage '*Vaya con Dios,*' from the song of the same name. Or perhaps I shall take an oath of silence. Poverty and chastity don't appeal as yet, but then I'm a very new recruit."

"I'm sure there'll be nothing resembling a soup-kitchen line," Mio said firmly. "This is a mad idea, Jim. I simply can't leave you here. You will *not* be able to eat. You will starve."

"My, but you do take a doomed view, my pigeon. You no longer wish me to slim down?"

"Tomorrow," Mio said, as to a small boy, "I'll return. At about noon. I'll bring groceries. By that time you'll know if you can possibly exist here. I'll park the car as near this spot as the sight-seers allow, and then I'll wander back down the road about fifty feet and turn left into the trees. I shall expect to find you there."

"You'll be followed, ducks."

"If I can't get away from them, I won't come. But I bet I manage it."

"Your small triumph over the hounds has gone to your head. But . . . maybe you *can* manage it. All right, thank you. It will be nice to see you. Something to look forward to, beyond the scholarly pursuits. I shall look forward *fervently*, in fact."

"That's touching and unusually gracious."

"How so? I've got a great interest in my stomach. And the first rule of mountain assaults is intelligent provisioning."

VIII

It was ten-thirty when Mio re-entered the lobby of the Arycasa. She was tired. And no wonder, she thought; she had been up since five-thirty that morning, driving almost without letup, and under the strain of Spanish roads and Spanish curves. And Cobham's Spanish sins. But . . . She stood indecisively in the small lobby and eyed the elevators that would take her to quiet room and soft bed, and then looked to her left. Through the lounge was the dining room, and she had had no dinner.

The headwaiter attempted to convey his inexpressible delight in having her back, and looked as if he meant it. He also remembered her wish to be inconspicuous, seated her at a small corner table, and left her studying a menu.

"Mrs. Heldon."

Mio leapt into mid-air, knocked over the water pitcher, thereby pulling the headwaiter, her table waiter, and a bus boy to her side, and altogether destroying any possibility of remaining inconspicuous. She said crossly to Davis, "This looks like a mob scene. Damn it."

114

"I didn't mean to startle you. I just——"

"No one ever means to startle me, it seems. I just leave them in one place, and then without warning they pop up a hundred miles away, and speak to me out of the sides of their mouths."

"The sides . . ." His handsome face showed more confusion than hers probably did, and that annoyed her. He had no right to look so slapped; it made her feel guilty, and *he* was the guilty one. He said, "I didn't mean to—to pop up. You were looking at the menu, I guess, and——"

"Sit down," she said. "For goodness' sakes, sit down! I feel as if I were in a forest. Thank you, Juan. It's quite dry enough. Just— May I have a glass of sherry, please? La Ina. Mr. Davis?" He nodded. "Two glasses, Juan."

The little crowd dispersed. Davis said, "I——"

"Where did you come from? How did you get here? *Why* did you come here?"

"We drove down together. The——"

"We?"

"Jones, West, and I."

"Well! The whole cast! There you all were Walachia-ing, or something, in S'Agaró, and all of a sudden a mass impulse came upon you to rush to Barcelona." She paused, giving him a chance to stammer so that she might interrupt him. But he didn't stammer. He was examining her quietly, a small smile creasing the corners of his eyes. "Well?" she demanded. "What are you doing here?"

He shook his head slowly. "At first," he said, "that wasn't very clear. Not to me, at any rate. But now—— We were pursuing you."

Inexplicably Mio abandoned the idea of asking why and said instead, "How did you find me?"

"That wasn't very difficult, Mrs. Heldon." His smile flickered away, and he said, "May I ask you a question? Do you know Jones? Had you met him before?"

"I had never met him before."

"I see." He looked at her steadily, the pale eyes enigmatically direct. "I asked because he was the—the propelling force in getting us here. He seemed almost maniacally disturbed by your absence. . . . Well—to start from the beginning—I normally have breakfast in my room, and during the few days I've known Westerland, so did he. And Cobham. So there usually wasn't anyone around at breakfast time. But this morning we all appeared. I showed up around ten; Jones was eating in the bar; West came along a few minutes later." He paused. "It was undoubtedly a direct compliment to you, Mrs. Heldon."

His stating of that compliment surprised Mio. But everything about Peter Davis surprised Mio somewhat. Most surprising were the combined facts that he was handsome, and quiet, and likable, qualities she considered mutually incompatible. Men of his—beauty—were rarely quietly likable. They presented challenges, by the sheer fact of their faces' existence. You cannot be unaware of me, such faces said; either you will pursue me or you will turn away a little too quickly to make it very clear that my appearance does not affect you, to make it crystal clear that you will *not* pursue me. The owners of these faces learned their power very young, when they got the extra lollipop from their aunts, when their teachers forgave them their homework, when they were worn out from trudging back and forth during their first game of Post Office. But Peter Davis seemed genuinely unaware of the effect that he created, and so the defensive or offensive attitude, whichever came unbidden to a woman, slipped quickly away.

"We waited around quietly enough," he said, "but I'm sure we were all absorbed in hoping *you* wouldn't take breakfast in *your* room. I—I was looking forward to saying good-by to you, at the least. And, too, I was hoping I might hitch that ride. But what we got for our patience was Ibáñez." Ibáñez had come rushing in, Davis explained, "all controlled politeness and restrained fury," and asked questions. He had been up all night, looking for Cobham, Ibáñez told them, and he was still looking. Davis pointed out that Cobham wasn't in their pockets, and Westerland said that it seemed most unlikely that S'Agaró was the place to look; wouldn't Cobham be miles away? Westerland had wanted to know. Ibáñez had responded to the effect that doubling back was not unheard of, and since Mrs. Heldon had doubled back, perhaps Cobham . . . ?

"That threw us into confusion, since we were assuming you were in your room. Ibáñez explained, and I imagine he explained rather more than he intended. He had just watched you drink coffee in the village, we gathered, and your calmness had apparently infuriated him. And you were going to Barcelona, and you had been almost to France, and he thought you had Cobham. West wanted to know why he didn't look—in your car, he suggested, or up your sleeve. Before Ibáñez could burst a polite blood vessel, Jones said haughtily that it was impossible for you to be involved with Cobham. I—frankly, I wondered how he could be so certain, and Ibáñez had no hesitation in asking. It—well, it turned into a brawl." He stopped, considered, and continued without defining the brawl: Ibáñez had spent another half hour, asking the same questions over and over again, and Jones had got into a fever of impatience. "I think he's a little screwy, and screwy impatience seemed to ooze out of him like—like mud." Davis looked a little surprised by his figure of speech, but he didn't correct it. "The minute Ibáñez left, apparently for Barcelona, Jones rushed for the door like a schoolboy given recess. But I held him up by asking where he was going."

Jones had shilly-shallied about answering, but it was clear to Davis that he was also en route to Barcelona. So Davis and Westerland had announced that they would go along. Jones tried but could find no way out of permitting them to accompany him. The inability had infuriated him, Davis said. Little purple veins had appeared on his pale face, and Davis thought he was going to have a fit. "And I mean it just that way," Davis added. "A real fit, epileptic, apoplectic, something like that. But he calmed down, and we paid our bills, and here we are." His long light gray eyes became almost involved in the smile he gave her, and she thought that perhaps her verdict had been wrong, that perhaps he did occasionally achieve warmth.

"How did you find me after you got here?"

"Easy enough to call the Ritz, the Avenida-Palace, and the Arycasa."

"And eighty smaller hotels and *pensions*."

"You wear your clothes with something I happen to like better than Parisian chic. But the clothes themselves are Parisian, I think."

The better the compliments to surprise me with . . . She gathered her courage and asked the pertinent question: "But *why*? Why did you follow me? The three of you. Leaving aside compliments."

"I can't speak for the others, Mrs. Heldon. Me? Well, I

was curious. And I like Cobham. Had a vague idea I might help in some way. And I can't leave aside the compliment and still answer your question because a large part of it was that I thought it would be nice to see you again." He waited. When she didn't say anything, he added, "Jones's reasons certainly weren't that simple. He acted as if finding you were a matter of life and death. That's why I asked if you knew him."

The waiter came and took her order. Davis said he had eaten.

Then Mio said, "Jones. He frightens me."

He nodded slowly.

"But why should he frighten me?"

"You probably sense that imbalance—that violence—that I feel in him."

"Venom. Yes. Well, I don't know Mr. Jones, I never saw him before"—she paused, came to a hesitant decision, and then picked her words carefully—"but I think I know something about him."

Davis arched a black eyebrow.

"From the newspapers. I remembered it during Ibáñez's little passport examination, when that lawyer business came up. A lawyer named Arthur Jones was disbarred a few years ago because he had done something illegal. It had to do with two divorces. They said he was dealing in extortion disguised as alimony."

"I don't remember anything like that."

"I found it particularly memorable because—well, among other things, the judge was unusually caustic. Apparently the man's threats had been very dreadful, worse than one would expect of a lawyer, of a man who wasn't really a—a gangster. The judge—implied an evil to him."

"Um. Well, I'd certainly find no difficulty in 'implying an evil' to our Jonesy. He seems so pallid and unimportant that when he does turn—malevolent—it's even more of a jolt. I'm surprised I don't remember the case. Perhaps I was already out of the country. Who were the men—the divorcés?"

"It was one man."

"But you said there were two divorces involved."

"It was—Charles Morningside."

"Oh." Inexplicably Davis seemed uncomfortable. Inexplicably he changed the subject: "And Cobham?"

Mio's still face didn't flicker. "Cobham?" she repeated blankly.

There *was* more life—and awareness of life—in Davis's glittering smile, although it still was not as infectious as Cobham's or Westerland's, each of whom grinned from a warmly derisive heart. He said, "All right. I'll accept that."

"What?"

" 'Cobham?' " he said, mimicking her innocent blandness. "Quite a guy, isn't he? I suppose you don't know what he's done, either? What Ibáñez is after him for?" Mio shook her head. "No, I thought not." The long eyes glittered in friendly mockery. "Well, if there were any way in which I could help him, I'd be glad to. For me, that's saying quite a lot, because I'm afraid I'm lazy. Not—not given to going out of my way, you know."

"No," Mio said, out of her continuing curiosity, "I don't know."

He obviously hadn't expected her to follow the comment up; he looked embarrassed. "Oh, I just mean I kind of take things as they come. Don't go out of my way looking for trouble. Or for anything else, for that matter."

"That means you are neither hunted nor hunter? Not a—Walachian?"

"*Sure* you haven't been exposed to Cobham lately? That's his refrain. And"—his smile died abruptly—"I don't find it so funny. Walachians, fleers—well, that could mean half the misfits in the world. Perhaps all the misfits. The spinsters, maybe. Their Walachia is the room or the small apartment all spotlessly clean and neat, ready for no one. And the playboys, rich and otherwise. The fifth drink is a ticket to Walachia. People who get psychoanalyzed, perhaps they're looking for a passport back to living lands, places that are still on the map. The murderers, the thieves, the sinners, the simply lonesome—aren't they all running and looking for a place to stop?"

"The lonesome?" Mio didn't know whether she was speaking to him or to herself. "You?" she asked.

He looked across the restaurant and she thought he wasn't going to answer. Then he said, "I have never been lonesome." He brought his eyes back to hers, but they were still vague. "Perhaps now I am. But Jim was wrong, back there in S'Agaró. The world isn't divided simply into categories of hunters and hunted. There are also the—drifters."

Was he talking about himself? Her confusion mounted. He had seemed lazy, but not purposeless. But then her picture of him was admittedly very vague and wavering of line. Perhaps because he himself, beneath the unmoving surface, was wavering of line? His was not a weak face. He was handsome but not pretty; he looked strong in a tensile way, and capable. Not capable in West's purposeful fashion, but . . . She asked, "You mean some people have no goals?"

"Well, not exactly. I should think everyone has a goal. To

want something. To want it enough—a great deal . . ." He stopped and his face muscles rippled. Mio felt a sympathetic tenseness in her jaw and realized that she was trying to help the face in its struggle to—to what? To express. To feel?

He slipped quickly back into impassive normality. He said negligently, "Perhaps the difference is most people know what their goals are, and the drifters don't. So unless it's forced on them they just sail through without either the content or discontent of normal people. All this isn't really my idea. Someone said something like it once, and it stuck in my mind."

"Was it West?"

He blinked. "Matter of fact, I think it was."

"You and West—you're really not friends, old acquaintances, something like that?"

"Just met him. As we told you. But we're—uh—compatible."

"Not at the moment, apparently. Where is he now—Mr. Westerland?"

Davis's grin got broader than usual, nearer the small-boyishness of Westerland's. "Mr. Westerland and Mr. Jones are closeted with the ubiquitous Señor Ibáñez. They may even be in jail, since they've been gone for hours."

"And how come you aren't with them?"

"I ducked. The three of us checked in, and before going up to our rooms agreed to come down and meet in the bar for a drink. West and I agreed, that is; Jones looked as if he disapproved but would grudgingly put up with it, although I don't recall that anyone asked him. Fifteen minutes later I put one foot out of the elevator, took a quick look at the view, stepped back in, and said, 'Arriba!' I must have put a lot of intensity into it because we shot up like a champagne cork. I got out on the top floor, sat in one of those nice soft chairs in the hall, and smoked several cigarettes."

"While they looked for you."

"Now, I wouldn't know about that. Since I wasn't in my room, I couldn't answer the phone or the door. And if they looked for me, no one thought of looking around the seventh floor. The elevator boy is richer by a hundred pesetas, so he and I are happy, at least."

Davis continued to smile. "You should have caught that glimpse of him and Jones in the lobby. They're both tall, and Ibáñez is amazingly diminutive. West is naturally calm, and although Jones seems to veer between pale calmness and apoplexy, he was having one of his pale minutes just then. Ibáñez was simply hopping, like a terrier, trying to surround them, and calling out instructions, directions, pleas, commands to the hotel desk and to people I couldn't see. It was very funny."

Mio sipped her coffee, picturing the scene. It must have been funny. Why, she wondered, had Ibáñez been angry? And the question answered itself easily: Everyone seemed to be converging on Barcelona and he must be feeling that he was up against an enormous, frustrating combination of foreigners. Enormous, frustrating foreigners. She smiled slightly, and then the smile faded. No matter what Ibáñez had concluded, those three men were *not* involved in hiding Cobham; she knew that as no one else could. So why were they here? Because of her, Davis had flatly admitted. Because they hadn't finished her off on the rainy road? The idea seemed infinitely childish. Besides Davis had actually said that it was Jones who was chasing her. Jones, a lawyer involved with the Morningside estate—no, he was not. He was no longer a lawyer and he couldn't be involved with

Charlie's cousins. They were the kind of people who passed large and stuffy legal firms from generation down to generation. Morningside—Jones—estate—divorces . . . something resembling a reason for Jones's presence and pursuit of her caught at the edge of her mind and was quickly dismissed. She did not want to think about it. And there might well be other reasons for Jones and Chris and Peter Davis to have come to Barcelona. There was no need to assume that Davis was telling the truth, or the whole truth. He had wanted to—to latch onto her previously, had asked for a ride, and in the opposite direction. And *someone* had all that illegal money. Cobham had been sure enough of that to rush to S'Agaró from Paris. And Cobham had thought it was money from the Astra robbery. And Cobham should know. But—who?

Her eyes moved up to Davis's and she found that his indolence had broken so far down that she could detect something uncomfortably like tender amusement. It flustered her, and then it worried her. Had her thoughts been readable? But that was impossible; passivity was her normal expression. Nevertheless she instinctively hit out against the dread possibility of invasion: "And what are you doing here in Spain, Mr. Davis?"

The baldness rocked him slightly; enough, she noted with satisfaction, to clear the amusement off his face. He said, "Please call me Peter." He added reminiscently, "That question was one of the first things you ever said to me."

"Yes." She waited.

"I'm vacationing."

"Two weeks with pay?"

"I've been here over a year."

Her curiosity was as high as ever but her courage was ebbing. Could she simply say, "And how do you support yourself?" No, she couldn't.

But he took pity on her. "Spain is cheap, you see. There are a lot of veterans like me over here, hanging around. Bumming around, if you prefer. It's a good place because our pensions stretch further."

It was an entirely new aspect and Mio faced it with confusion. "Pensions? But don't you have to be wounded to get a pension?"

"Well, yes. You're quite generous about it, though, you taxpayers. For instance, I am considered totally disabled. Just because I have only one leg."

IX

THE PHONE DIDN'T AWAKEN MIO, BUT IT DID DIS-
turb her. She had pushed slowly up through successive
layers of semi-blackout until, at about eight o'clock, she arrived at a happy medium. Then she lay, neither asleep nor
awake, and contemplated the light pattern cast on the ceiling by the Spanish jalousies—very satisfactory affairs, somewhat like venetian blinds, hung on the outside of the
windows but operated from the inside. They combined the
functions of blind, shutter, and awning—controlling the air,
light, and sun intake. They also made for interesting Georgia
O'Keeffe shadow effects.

Then the phone had started to ring, and it rang, it
seemed to Mio, constantly.

First the desk clerk wanted to know if she wished breakfast in her room, and when Mio said no, with a certain forcefulness, he removed himself hurriedly. Now, that, Mio
thought, replacing the receiver, was strange. Never before in
Spain, or anywhere else for that matter, had anyone disturbed her to ask if she wished to eat. They normally as-

sumed, without particular flattery, that she would know when she wished to eat. She then concluded that Ibáñez or one of his associates wanted to make sure she hadn't already left the building, by the service exit, perhaps. That reminded her that today was the day she would be grilled. Being grilled on the subject of causing sequined panties to be given away should have been funny, but she didn't look forward to it. The service exit began to seem like rather a good idea, and she decided, as if she had spent her life coming and going by unorthodox routes, that she must investigate it.

The next call was even stranger. To her slightly impatient "*Digame!*" a flat, arrogant voice said, "Oh, sorry. I must have the wrong room."

"Whom did you want?"

"Mrs.—Heldon."

The hesitation brought added vigor to her voice. "This is Mrs. Heldon."

"Oh, hello. Good morning."

"Who is this?"

"This is Arthur Jones."

That surprised her into total wakefulness. She said warily, "Good morning, Mr. Jones."

"Good morning. Peter Davis told me that you were here."

Then the conversation died. It can't die yet, Mio thought; it hasn't lived. She held the receiver away from her ear, looked at it curiously, and then tried out the mouthpiece: "Are you still there, Mr. Jones?"

"Yes. Yes. I was—that is, I was wondering if you had eaten yet?"

Oh no! "I have not eaten yet. I do not intend to eat yet. I am not hungry yet. But may I ask why *you* ask?"

127

His voice was pale and hesitant: "I just—just thought maybe you would . . . maybe we could, would, meet in the dining room."

"Oh. Well, I'll be down in about an hour. If you're there we'll probably meet."

"Yes. Well, then, I'll see you there. Good-by."

That made it sound as if she had made a date, Mio thought, replacing the receiver. Then she recoiled toward the other side of the bed as if the telephone were a black snake. *With Arthur Jones?*

The phone rang. Mio looked at it, looked at the patterned ceiling, and got leisurely out of bed.

The bath water satisfactorily drowned the sound.

But the next time it rang she was out of the tub. She picked the thing up cautiously and, the caution in her tone, tried two languages: "*Dígame?* Hello?"

Peter Davis's voice was deeply pleasant. "Hi," he said. "Good morning! Isn't it a nice morning?"

"I don't know. I haven't tried it yet."

"Well, you should. You must. You went off so quickly last night that I really didn't get a chance to make some suggestions. If you haven't seen them, there are some wonderful sights in and around Barcelona. How about riding down to Sitges? And you should see Mount Tibidabo. And Montserrat."

She caught her breath and then tried to cover the gasp by speaking quickly: "I've seen them all, thank you, Mr. Davis. Peter," she added, to soften the abruptness of the refusal. "And I have to do some shopping this afternoon anyway."

"I see." The drawling voice contained an unusual note of regret. "Well, how about breakfast?"

Mio choked. She recovered and said, "Fine. Half hour in the dining room?"

"Good! See you there." He disconnected.

Mio put on a suit skirt, and then, with quiet resignation, answered the phone.

"This is Chris Westerland. How have you been during our long separation?"

"I've survived the whole thirty-six hours."

"Forty-eight, I make it. Haven't actually seen you in that long, and my survival is in doubt. How about——"

"*Eating!*" Mio said, on a low shrieking note.

There was a pause, and then Westerland chuckled. The sound was so reminiscent of Cobham that Mio felt a flash of something like lonesomeness. "Been bombarded with invitations, have you?"

"Even from the desk clerk."

That stopped him, but only momentarily. "The desk clerk?" he repeated. "Oh, you think they were checking?"

"Peter tells me you are even pal-ier with the little señor than I am. What do you think?"

"I think that if you are going to live outside the law——"

"I——"

"Don't answer!" Westerland said quickly. "This wire is probably as alive and well tenanted as a flophouse bed. And if you insist upon offering, uh, aid and comfort . . . you will continue to receive a good deal of attention from the little señor."

"And from Mr. Jones?"

"Ah, now that." He did sound so much like Cobham, she thought. Their voices were slightly higher than Davis's, with a pleasant, musical timbre and a note of humor that seemed constantly present. . . . And then the humor left

Westerland's voice. "Jones," he said with an effect of carefulness, "is a different matter. It's something I would like to
discuss with you. If you trust me at all, sort of as a fellow-
traveler and fellow-American. You should certainly discuss
it with *someone*. But not on this phone. And that reminds
me, by fellow-traveler"—the humor came back with full
force—"I intended to convey the meaning that two people
are moving together in space. No political overtones."

Mio laughed.

"Now, this discussion can take place—where?"

"Breakfast."

"Certainly. Sooner the better. But I gather it's going to be
a mass meal. So how about this afternoon?"

"I have to do some shopping."

"More lingerie with spangles?"

"Oh dear. He does tell everything he knows, doesn't he?
Most unpolicemanlike."

"Now, now, don't let's make him madder. I think fury
itself explains why he's giving so much out. He's lost con-
trol. Of everything—the people, the situation, his temper.
Let's smooth his lot by telling him where we'll be this afternoon at cocktail time, shall we? How about the Ritz at five?"

"Good. I'll see you there."

"See you first in the crowded dining room."

The three men were there before her, and they rose together. They were good-looking men, especially in a body;
they were well mannered; they were strangely unstrange to
her. She remembered how she had assessed them as a worth-
catching group, a bag a woman could be pleased with. And
she remembered Cobham's reply. His so-accurate reply.
Now they were more than good-looking men; they were

three quarters of a whole that comprised one thief, black-marketeer variety; one larger-scale type; one or more probable pursuers—or did she think that just because Cobham so often seemed to be right? And although they seemed oddly familiar, despite the short time she had spent with them, they presented four larger enigmas than the complete strangers had. But that was not odd, because one had to know a man, even somewhat, before being confused by him. And the group now consisted of four partly known, realigned factors—Davis's laziness reassessed, if only to the point of a deeper confusion, his handsomeness established and so robbed of its shock quality; Jones re-evaluated from a pale, haughty man to a violently arrogant one, from a surface nothingness to a queer and turbulent depth; Westerland grown from boyish good-naturedness to an adult capable of very quick thinking, and his ability to irritate her dimly recognized as a defense against her response to his strength. And Cobham, awaiting her on a mountaintop—the realization overtook Mio, the friendless, with startling force— Cobham was a dear friend, to be forgiven as one would a brother no matter what his sins. And the word "brother" seemed well fitting. She had never had a brother, and she had always felt the lack. Cobham, on the other hand, did have a sister, one he included among his "loved ones." She was a much-divorced sister. The thought seemed to forge a link between the sister and Mio. . . . She was brought up short by the realization that the idea was insanely farfetched.

Mio listened, and said little, while the men talked, Westerland doing most of it. Westerland described his and Jones's hours in the station house. He had evidently found the experience—which he explained as a series of repetitive, aimless questionings punctuated by long, boring waits—extremely funny. Jones was just as evidently not amused.

No one asked her about Cobham. But there was an air of acceptance, as if they all knew she had him, as Westerland had put it, up her sleeve. She pictured the stark mountain and thought, Time to go up my sleeve. She put out her cigarette and said, "If you will all excuse me . . ."

"Ah yes. Shopping, I think you said, Mrs. Heldon?" Jones's pale eyes were nasty.

Westerland laughed. "Not the Jorba again, I hope? These things never work twice, believe me."

"Believe you, Mr. Westerland? Do you speak from a depth of experience?"

His smile broadened. "You're beginning to sound like a mixture of Cobham and the little señor. I just hope that you *have* a good plan, that you——"

"I am going shopping," Mio said firmly. "*Hasta la tarde.*" She felt, as she walked through the big dining room, that the eyes of the three standing figures behind her were hungry eyes in a far less flattering fashion than a woman might wish.

In her car, around the corner from the hotel, she pulled on her gloves thoughtfully. Westerland was entirely right, of course; a plan would be a nice thing to have. A good plan would be even better. But she had shot her bolt the day before. The Jorba had been her one stroke of genius, and even if that had not been worn out by usage, it would not have worked today since she could not walk to Montserrat. So she was simply going to try to shake her pursuers, whom she suspected were the gentlemen in the car parked on the opposite side of the street and all the way back on the other side of the Calle de Gerona. It was, she thought, giving the gauntlets a small final tug, truly ridiculous to try to shake a police car in its own milieu. And so the attempt would fail. Then she would put her alternate, but uncomfortable, plan into action: shake them on foot, and take a bus.

However . . . She pulled the starter.

Jones said, "What is that idiot woman trying to do? She's not trying to duck that carful of cops just by driving around, for God's sake? Does she think she knows this city better than they do?"

"She obviously knows it better than you do." As Jones braked furiously, Westerland, who had been perched on the edge of his seat, braced himself against the dividing upholstery to keep from pitching headfirst into the front. "And *I* know it better than you do, chum. Couldn't you tell there'd be a light there? I wish you'd let me drive."

Davis was sitting comfortably back on the rear seat as if enjoying a sight-seeing tour. He said easily, "Might not be a bad idea, Jones. West knows——"

"May I point out that you two were not invited? If you're going to continue to force yourselves on me, at least do me the favor to shut up. . . . God damn it!" He pulled violently right and just missed the bumper of the trolley bus ahead of him. "Did you ever see so many squares in your life? Squares! The Diagonal is diagonal, Cataluña is pentagonal, the Plaza de Calvo Sotelo is circular, Universidad is—is——" He choked.

"A mess?" Davis offered.

"—and so they stick up three-way lights, and 'one way only' signs and——"

"Don't you understand?" Westerland sounded impatient.

"She's doing it deliberately. Picking the most confusing *plazas*. And rushing from one to another. It's not such a bad idea. Doesn't matter how well the cops know the city, they might run afoul of one of those lights, and then she'd be off and away. I think it's a good try."

"They're police!" Jones's voice had a nasty snarl. "They're authority! If you've no respect for authority, the Barcelonans certainly have. The police don't have to wait for the lights. They'll just——"

"Don't be silly," Davis said, but his usual calm tone robbed the words of sting. "All the authority in the world wouldn't prevent a crash if anyone tried to skip one of those lights at this hour in this traffic. West is right. She stands a chance. And"—his slow voice quickened—"there she goes!"

Almost two blocks ahead of them the little Citroën caught the tail end of a yellow light, went through the Diagonal (its third time around that particular statue that morning), passed the Parellada Restaurant, and turned sharp left. The police car, almost immediately behind the Citroën, attempted to jump the now red light, snarled instantly into a mass of cars, and drew the policeman from the statue's base to its side. The traffic cop tried frantically to release his colleagues, but it took him a full minute. Then the police sedan shot to the next corner and belatedly followed the Citroën in a left turn.

"Well." Westerland sounded resigned. "She didn't have such a bad plan after all, did she, Jones?"

"She'll never make it!" Jones's hands on the wheel were spastic with rage. The side of his face that the two men in the rear could see was twitching as if overcome by a furious attack of ague. "She's in the open now," he said, his voice shaking as uncontrollably as was the rest of him. "All the streets between here and the Universidad are wide and even. The Universidad is the nearest confusing spot and they'll catch up before she gets there. But *we* haven't got a chance. We——"

Davis's infrequent laugh was shocking against the rage with which Jones had filled the car. "You got it wrong, Jones," he said. "*This* is the nearest *plaza.*"

"What the hell does that mean? We can't turn left in this tangle!"

"No. Let's turn right." Davis waved indolently toward the left. "Because, see?"

On the Paseo de Gracia the second car in the stream facing the Diagonal, waiting for the light and the final clearance of traffic, was a small, familiar Citroën.

"Doubled back, by heaven!" Westerland said. "Smart girl! Well!" The smile returned to his voice. "She's smart enough, Jones, so that you had better lag a hell of a distance back. If she keeps on in the direction she's now aiming at we'll have fairly clear roads. Three blocks behind her, at the least, Jones—because she's a smart girl."

The direction she was aiming at was Montserrat.

They were on the quiet, shaded main street of the village of Martorell when Davis put it into words. "We're going to Montserrat, don't you think?"

"Or somewhere short of or beyond there." Westerland apparently didn't believe in jumping to conclusions.

"I'll bet on Montserrat. Come to think of it, I suggested we go sight-seeing up there today. She sounded startled. Now I can see why."

"Pull up!" Westerland said urgently. "Jones! She's stopping!"

Jones pulled his car to the side of the road and parked behind a truck. "I don't see," he said, "why you keep referring to 'her.' We're so far behind that car that it could be full of monkeys. The most popular car in Spain," he said in his prissy, precise, toneless voice, with its nasty undernote, "is the Citroën. Especially black Citroëns."

"It's Mio." Westerland was soothing. "I'm pretty good at keeping my eyes on a moving object like that. Relax."

"Good at trailing?" Davis sounded amused.

"Well, no better than you." Westerland returned his smile.

"She's coming out," Jones said. "Out of that *bodega*. See? With the stuff in her arms. It *is* she," he added grudgingly, and maneuvered the car from behind the truck.

X

WHEN, HALF AN HOUR LATER, THEY ARRIVED AT
the plateau on which the monastery stood, and caught up
with the Citroën—parked and empty—Jones turned in his
seat with a snarling ferocity so unexpected that Westerland
moved backward. "You're so God damned smart!" he said.
His voice cracked. "So we stayed well behind her! And where
is she now?"

In the silence that followed the two men in the back instinctively retreated before an intensity that reached malig-
nantly out toward them. Then Davis said quietly, "What's
the difference?"

Jones's face worked convulsively. He forced his mouth
open, closed it abruptly, and then faced forward, his whole
body quivering.

Westerland picked the question up. "Yes," he said. "What
is the difference? Why are we here, anyway? I thought——"

"You're here because you don't know when you're not
wanted! You forced your way into my car, just as you did in
S'Agaró!"

"Then, why are *you* here? I thought the idea was to find out where Cobham was. And in general we have accomplished that; he's on Montserrat. As for Mio Heldon, she'll return to her car, of course, so——"

"While we're asking idle questions," Davis said, "why do we care *where* Cobham is?"

Westerland turned in his seat. "You don't?"

"Not in the least. Were you interested because you thought I was interested? Whither I goest? Now, that's funny, because I thought I was following you and that *you* were interested in Cobham. *I* thought maybe *you* thought ——" He stopped and then said lazily, "That sentence is too confusing to bother with."

Westerland examined him expressionlessly. Then he turned his attention to Jones's back. "I find Jones far more confusing. I don't——"

Jones swiveled in his seat. His face was passive and pale and his voice had regained the monotony that served it for normality. "My interest is none of your business," he said arrogantly but with an unanswerable air of logic, "—is it? Now, either we drop the discussion or you must both get out of my car."

Silence took over again. Then Westerland said, "Let's look at the joint now that we're here." It was tacit acceptance of an inability to argue with logic plus another, not so easily definable reaction.

"I've seen the monastery." Jones leaned forward and clasped his hands on the top of the steering wheel with an effective air of digging in for the duration.

Davis said, "So have I, but I'll go along with you." He directed his next words at the back of Jones's head, "If you won't drive off and leave us?"

"When the Morningside woman returns I shall follow her. But I'll give her a head start, so if you want to take the chance . . ." His shoulders moved upward in a brief shrug.

"Come on," Westerland said. "We'll keep an eye out."

As they walked across the parking lot toward the stairs that led up to the monastery, Davis indicated the car with a brief motion of his head. "It isn't his rages that bother me," he said, "as much as the quickness of his recoveries. It doesn't seem—possible. It doesn't seem . . ." He searched for the word.

Westerland supplied it. "Normal." He stopped in the middle of the path and looked back. Davis turned with him. "It *isn't* normal," Westerland added. "You know, we shouldn't go off like this."

"You mean we'll get left? Well, there are always busses. But if you feel that way, why did we get out of the car? It was your idea, you know. I've seen the place."

"Yeah. But his—abnormality—suddenly made the car seem too small. I just wanted to get away from him." He turned abruptly to face Davis. "You wouldn't mind losing him?"

Davis didn't appear to be startled by the abruptness. He smiled slowly. "Not in the least," he said. "How about you?"

"Then it's the Morningside girl?"

"Well, I think she's pretty."

"And rich."

"Don't be silly, West. For that matter, you seem rather taken by her yourself." He paused, but Westerland said nothing; he was staring at the distant blur that was the back of Jones's neck. Davis added, "I wish that when Ibáñez was in that towering rage in S'Agaró yesterday morning he had given out a little about Cobham and Jones the way he did about Mio."

"He was maddest at Mio. She had offended his Spanish assumption that women do not move without male permission. But"—Westerland smiled sweetly—"I think I have Cobham spotted." The smile faded. "It's Jones I can't place."

"Then we can swap. I have a little on Jones. Okay?"

Westerland regarded him levelly. Then he said, "Cobham would probably be a black-market operator."

Davis laughed. "A type you just naturally recognize, huh? Well, Jones is an ex-lawyer. Disbarred."

"Oh? And is that in *your* field of recognition?"

"Mio told me. He was connected with Morningside in some way. Over the business of a divorce—what else? And she used a strange phrase—the judge, she said, 'implied an evil' to Jones."

"Smart judge. 'Evil' is the word for Jonesy." Westerland frowned. "And if we admit to being fond of the girl, I think we shouldn't take a chance of leaving her at the mercy of evil."

"We're not on a desert island, West. Have you looked around?" Davis nodded at the dozens of cars parked in front of them, and waved a languid hand to indicate the people— a mixed and colorful group of Spanish and tourists, drawn to the thousand-year-old fastness by the tourist's desire to see everything; by the beauty lover's wish to look up to the Pyrenees, towering in the north, and down to the river Llobregat, distantly sparkling in the winter sun; by the seekers after the past, who would warm to the rumors of the Holy Grail and to the long history of Our Sacred Lady of Montserrat; by those who liked to harrow up their spines, and who would therefore investigate the caves, and stare with obsessive awe at the fantastically and frightfully carved precipices that looked like demons and animals the earth has never known; and by the simply religious, who came, by automobile, funicular, and bus to pay homage to the little black Virgin. Davis added dryly, "Mio is not exactly alone, wherever she is."

"I suppose not." Westerland was still staring at Jones's back. "And neither of them is connected with—us—in any way, it would seem." He sounded dubious.

"Aren't they? Are you telling me or asking me? And what is 'us'?"

Westerland laughed.

Davis said, "To quote you, we're a happy bunch of Walachians. Well, do we sight-see, or do we return to that nut?"

"Let's look around inside, but let's keep an eye on the outside. One of us can stick near a window. Then if we need to we can get out, down the terrace, and to the car in about one minute flat."

"Okay. And you mustn't miss the view."

"I'm looking at the view." Westerland swung his arm in a wide circle to take in the Pyrenees, the Mediterranean, the low-lying Spanish countryside.

"Yeah, but if you walk over to that low stone wall at the edge of the parking space, you can look straight down a couple of thousand feet. Quite a sight."

"I'll take a look before we get back into the car. Come on."

Cobham peered coyly from behind a tree, and then swapped coyness for an exaggerated furtiveness.

Mio said, "You look like Friar Something in an extremely bad Shakespearean repertory production."

"Friar Laurence in *Romeo and Juliet*—the marrying one? He was a very nice character; very well spoken. But he was a Franciscan."

"No. More like Friar Rush."

Cobham hung his head and remained behind the tree as if too crushed to blossom forth.

"And if you're under any mad impression that that tree is a hiding place, let me advise you that bits of black habit are bulging out on all sides."

Cobham emerged, turned, and contemplated the tree, his head cocked toward his shoulder. "'Tis but a sapling, and I am a man full-grown." Keeping his eyes on the tree, he reached absently out with his right hand and relieved Mio of her brown paper bag. "When it reaches man's estate . . ." His words got lost in an apple.

"If it eats like you, it'll be the first redwood on Montserrat."

Cobham managed to anchor the apple with his teeth, grin over it, and peel an orange at the same time.

"Don't litter," Mio said. "You should feel proprietary by now." She sat down on a mossy patch, placed the contents of the bag in a neat row, and put the orange peelings in the empty paper bag.

Cobham dropped down beside her with a grunt and eyed the assorted meats through their individual oiled-paper wrappings. He gave another grunt, of satisfaction this time, and said, "Very nice. And the paper bag is a tribute to your beauty. Did the *bodega dueño* have to send out for it?"

"I asked nicely."

"I'll wager. And did you ask the bobbies nicely not to follow you?"

"Them? Oh, I just left them." She gave an airy wave.

"I worry about this increasing facility of yours. Sincerely.
But"—he looked at the meats again—"it does come in
handy."

"How about you? Have you been facile?"

"I shall manage nicely, thank you. Did you know that this
place sleeps five thousand? The guesthouses alone can put
up two thousand, and they put them up without the breath
of a question. When one leaves he contributes what he feels
he can afford, but the Benedictines wouldn't dream of asking for anything. Trouble is, those guesthouses seem to be
for the laity. I'm not sure that I wouldn't raise a question
by trying to move in. Incidentally, it's a pretty charming
laity, ducks. Enormous percentage of honeymooners. Isn't
it a lovely Spanish notion to spend one's honeymoon in, or
on, the doorstep of a monastery? They come to pray to the
little dark Virgin to bless their union, and they also come
because they are left so thoroughly alone. Benedictines apparently take an oath of non-curiosity——"

"That defrocks you before you start."

"—and I have twice passed myself vaguely off as a visiting
monk. Spent the morning in the library. Very famous library,
you know. Very instructive. Number of books in English,
too. And I have plans, sharpened by hunger, toward eating.
I shall march bravely into the hotel. All will be well, and
this must be your last trip, ducks. I plan to stay only a week,
perhaps less." He tackled some bologna. "And, let's admit
it, this is basically my natural habitat." He lost himself in
bologna.

"Yes, I think it is." Mio's voice was unexpectedly serious.

Behind his facial screen of bologna, Cobham's eyebrows could be seen to jump upward. "The wood, I mean, not the friar's life. Although Friar Rush wasn't too far from it. The devil disguised as a friar, the Fallen Angel."

"Upon second examination, that's sweet of you, ducks. I quite like that picture."

Mio continued to examine him, head tilted, face grave. "When I first set eyes on you the word 'faun' came to my mind."

"My pointed ears?" He fingered an ear, which was as round as the rest of him. "Or"—he developed a lascivious leer—"would you be confusing your terms a little? A satyr, perhaps?"

A small smile appeared on Mio's still face. "Perhaps I *am* confused. Maybe I mean a brownie, a sprite, a fairy." She paused to enjoy his excellent portrayal of speechless horror. "A wood nymph, then?" she suggested. "A dryad?"

"No, no, *no*, ducks! The nymph and dryad come only in the feminine gender. Perhaps you're thinking of a Druid. They were natural philosphers, like myself, religious men like myself, mysterious, and, like myself, British."

Mio laughed. "And, like you, given to human sacrifice."

"Little did you realize, but as a result of all these slanderous suggestions you have given me every moral right to tell you what I think of *your* appearance. And I shall. Prepare yourself." He paused, and then added sadly, "But I'm afraid it won't serve as reprisal. You are very beautiful, you know. A small, grave beauty with a bewitching serenity. Beyond this point in the discussion I dare not go lest I sink helplessly into a mire of all the clichés ever writ or spoke. I will *not* compare you to the cornflower crossed with the orchid, and the like. So there."

144

"Why, Jim! As a maker of such pretty speeches, I can't think how you remained a bachelor."

"Simple enough. I never thought or spoke thusly before. For you, my dear, I would consider renouncing half the joy, two thirds of the fun, and all of the adventure—or whatever my proportions were. And I'd do it with the happy suspicion that I was losing nothing and gaining much. If."

Mio's face was too well schooled in impassivity to betray her surprise. She clutched at the last word, as she imagined she was intended to. "If?"

"If you would grow up and give up your childish fear. There is nothing to fear, nothing to run from in life as you have lived it. Simply accept that and start living."

"Simple as that."

He nodded. "Exactly as simple as that. You merely have to accept it, which is not simple at all. But it would be easier done if you were not alone."

The surprise was still with Mio. She said, with a small laugh, "A minute ago you said you—that I was not very desirable in my present—frightened condition. So it's that old circle—you won't take me until I lose the fear, but you think I could lose the fear more easily if—if I had help."

"Well, I'd be big about it. Take you on, fear and all. Guide you out of Walachia. . . . I'm getting rather tired of that symbol."

"My dear." Mio paused. "That's very nice of you." She smiled. "Noble, in fact. But whether you're tired of the symbol or not, aren't you rather embroiled in the fact?" She waved at their surroundings.

"Yes. Yes, I am. I would remove myself."

"From the wood? Or from black-marketeering?" There

was more to the question, and the unspoken words hung in the air.

Cobham answered them. "I would renounce fear. With the same oversimplified cure-all that I mouthed at you. For you I would strike out or, if the necessity arose, accept a blow. Or blood. Or death."

"My dear Jim." Mio felt confused and inadequate, and it was clear that Cobham saw it. He talked on, largely, she thought, to give her time.

"It sounds, as I said, oversimplified. And, of course, it is, but that's partly because I'm not a very good Druid. A philosopher could explain, I should think, what I mean. That people like us are different from others only because the others have found a reason, and we haven't. If we find it, and it's not too late, we can change a little."

"If it's not too late. But what keeps it from being too late?"

"I don't know. The desire itself to find something is perhaps enough."

"Peter Davis said something like this. About a reason for being."

"Did he, now? When?"

"Last night. Oh, I haven't told you. They all came to Barcelona, to the Arycasa." Cobham adopted an expression of transparent fascination, and she explained. She ended the story with: "They came in Jones's car, and Jones seemed to have been the one who was doing the chasing."

"Of me?"

"Ostensibly. Really, of me."

"Why?"

She stirred restlessly, and felt of the moss, testing for dampness. Then she told him briefly what she suspected, what she was almost certain about, of Jones's past. When

146

she had finished, she assembled the bits of paper and carefully wrapped the remnants of Cobham's meal. "He frightens me," she added. She looked up and smiled. "Another fear."

"Ah, but different. Fear of the concrete but unknown. Your usual flight, on the other hand, is of the known and most unconcrete. I must say Jones disturbs me too. When he sat down at the table in S'Agaró he stared at you with never a blink. At first I thought it was the tribute that I was giving you myself, but in his case there was something added. Something I didn't like a bit. At the time I had a thought that I quite forgot in the ensuing excitement. But it comes back now: I thought he might have followed you to S'Agaró."

"I had never seen him before," Mio protested.

"One does not necessarily see a follower." Cobham got up and examined a bush. Then he turned around and stared through Mio. "What would he want of you—Mr. Arthur Jones?"

"I don't know."

Cobham was not listening. "He would probably like to be reinstated as a lawyer." He focused. "You couldn't have anything to do with that?"

"Goodness, no, Jim. I had nothing whatever to do with it."

"No. What, then? What do people want of other people? Money? Revenge?"

"I can think of no reason to give him money. And why would he want to be revenged on me?"

"Just because you *have* money? Or because you had a connection with Morningside? His connection with Morningside brought him disgrace; yours brought you money."

"And disgrace," Mio said bitterly.

"Not in his eyes. And, look you: you wouldn't be expected to *give* him money—he might be thinking of obtaining it from you. By blackmail? It seemed to me—even before I knew who you were—that *he* knew who you were."

"Yes. I was sure of it. I just—didn't think about it."

"Like Scarlett O'Hara? Well, let's think about it. Blackmail?"

"That's silly. I'm not *that* afraid of—of disclosure. I'd just move on if he disclosed my name."

"Yes. True." He paced a short measure between a tree and a bush.

"There was something in that will. . . ." Mio wrinkled her smooth forehead.

Cobham stopped short and ignored the fact that his habit had caught on the bush. "What, for goodness' sakes?"

"Well, I didn't pay too much attention to it. I just—just ran."

"Well, pay attention now. Try to remember."

"That is just what I've been avoiding. I have been carefully not thinking—of Charlie, wills, thirteen million dollars I don't want, courtroom scenes, or newspaper headlines."

"Drop it, ducks. Stop it. Open your mind. And your memory. I don't like that man either. And if he's up to something, better to know what and why. Would he be the lawyer for Morningside's cousins? No, he's no longer a lawyer."

"I thought of that. Anyway, they wouldn't have him. They're—solid, you know?"

He nodded, understanding. "Well, then if anything happened to you and the money reverted to the cousins, it wouldn't do him any good so——"

"The money wouldn't go to Charlie's cousins, anyway."

"No?" He tore impatiently at the bush, gathered his robe around him, and sat down facing Mio. "To whom would it go? Charity?"

"No." Mio looked down at the leaf she was tearing to pieces. "I don't know why it embarrasses me; it just seems to make me—sillier than ever. If I predeceased him or died before the will went through—through probate"—she raised her eyebrows queryingly and Cobham nodded agreement with her choice of the word—"then the money was to be divided equally between those other ex-wives of his who were still living."

Cobham stared at her.

Mio stared back, uncomprehendingly. "So," she said lamely, "the cousins wouldn't get it, you see?"

"*I* see, ducks. It's *you* who don't see. For goodness' sakes, Mio, don't go blind in this matter. It's perfectly clear now, and childishly simple. Jones was involved with two ex-wives, wasn't he? There are what—seven living?"

"Seven others."

Cobham's voice held the first sharp note she had ever heard there. "Drop it!" he said. "It's time for facing up. Two out of seven is more than a quarter. Almost a third of thirteen million dollars."

"But he's no longer a lawyer."

"What has that got to do with it? He no longer has so much to lose, that's all. And if you're thinking of those women—well, they were certainly unprincipled, weren't they? Almost by definition, no? So suppose he went to them and said, 'It didn't work last time but I'll make it work this time. And for more money. If I can get you almost two million dollars apiece, will you give me a fat percentage?' They wouldn't hesitate, would they? And he probably ap-

149

proached them separately. No witnesses. And if one welshed, he'd have the other to fall back on. Not," Cobham added grimly, "that they'd be likely to welsh, in view of his, by then, proven abilities."

"Jim," Mio whispered, "he wants to murder me?"

Cobham looked at her and then away. His graphic features showed his dilemma—he was transparently caught between the wish to soothe and reassure and the opposite need to awaken her to her danger. He finally said, "Well, now, ducks—it could be so. Maybe not murder, really, but . . ." Her expression stopped him. He said sharply, "What is it?"

"You don't know." She was still whispering. "We never told the others."

"Who's 'we'? What others? What *is* it?"

"West and I. We didn't explain to you or Peter. Or to Ibáñez or any of the police. You don't know how I really came to meet West." And then she told him of her near-brush with the sea, and the anonymous car that had been at fault.

She had barely finished before he was on his feet. "Well," he said with a kind of furious energy, "that settles it, doesn't it?" He started to remove his cassock.

"What are you doing?"

"Coming with you," Cobham said grimly from the depths of black cotton.

"Wait, Jim! It doesn't *have* to have been Jones. It could——"

"Could have been coincidence? Really, Mio! Maybe we couldn't prove it to a court or a cop, but it has been very thoroughly proved to me."

"But what good will it do me for you to go to prison?"

"I'm not going to have you alone around that madman."

"Alone? What about Ibáñez, and West and Peter and the other two million people in Barcelona?"

"Ibáñez seems pretty ineffectual to me. Anyway, he doesn't know anything about it, and you seem set against telling him. Not that it would do much good. He's concentrating on finding *me*, and he's probably not fond of you at the moment. And West and Peter are enigmas, dangerous enigmas. And those census figures you rattle off are compiled by a cross-eyed man who sees triple and has a knack for counting the legs of people who are passing through and multiplying by ten."

"Jim, will your rushing into jail change matters for better or worse? *You* think for a minute."

Cobham's head came back up through the black folds. Then he nodded slowly. "Yes. Makes sense, doesn't it? All right. I'll walk you to the edge of the wood. Then you go down the mountain and never again until the end of this week are you to be alone for a single instant. You understand? In your room, you lock the door. At all other times you seek people. Don't go out, even in the car, alone. Don't walk down the corridor to the elevator unless you hear people in the halls. Understand?"

"And at the end of the week?"

"I'll come down. I'll meet you in the Las Siete Puertas at noon a week from today, and then"—his voice slowed—"you'll come with me?"

Mio looked up at his face. It was a face she liked very much. She said, "I don't know. I don't—know."

He nodded. "You think about it. If you don't want to—visit Majorca, well, we'll fix up some other way to get you away from Jones. Far away." He put his hands down toward her in an invitation to stand, and she took them. As he pulled her to her feet, he said lightly, "We'll be clever and devious. My, yes." His voice sobered. "Meanwhile, my dear, you will take care?"

She nodded. "You too."

"I shall leave that to Montserrat." His voice remained grave. "I learned a poem here. A hymn. Sung at vespers. Would you like to hear it?"

She nodded again.

He said:

> "Rosa d'abril, Morena de la serra
> De Montserrat, estel
> Illuminau la cataláña terra,
> Guiau-nos cap al cel.

Do you understand it?"

"It's part French. Catalan? But I think I get the gist. 'Rose of April, Dark One of the Mountain of Montserrat, Bright Star of Catalan soil, Lead us up to heaven.'"

"That's it, in general."

"But not to heaven, Jim. Stay on earth, please."

He smiled. "I always oblige a lady." He took her hand and started leading her through the trees.

At the edge of the wood he said, "You know, my little pigeon, you quite owe it to me to stay on earth yourself. Remember that you're my passport out."

She felt a stab of disappointment. "Traveling with me would make it so much easier for you to get out of Spain?"

"No, ducks. Out of Walachia."

XI

Mio stepped into the sun and bustle and saw neither. She walked slowly past her car and sat on the low stone wall that clung to the brink of depth and distance. She looked down the sheer drop into the placid valley as if it were the column of ten steep years. With a common sense that was frightening in its clarity and obviousness she saw those years as cumulative idiocy. Everything she had felt, everything she had told herself, every excuse she had made could be bolstered and explained and even, to some degree, excused. But why make the excuses, why build the barrier? She *had* been embarrassed, humiliated, hurt, a score and more of times—all true—and just another excuse. Flight had not helped the situation; it had not even removed her from it since she took all the hurt and humiliation with her.

Cobham had apologized for oversimplification, but Mio felt that in some instances it was a beautiful quality. If she could continue this oversimplification of her problem, it would reduce itself almost to nothingness. Then she had only to deal with it simply—to put up with it as a nuisance not worth the flinching from, to——

"Hello, Mrs.—Heldon."

She looked up from the valley with a far greater sensation of breathless fear than any discovery of her identity had ever brought her. It seemed to her that after her heart had thundered furiously, once, and her blood had leapt so spasmodically forward that she heard and felt the rush, and her breath had gulped convulsively inward without her conscious aid, all three quite literally stopped functioning. Then her muscles were transmuted to fluid and she quickly put a hand beside and behind her to serve as a brace and keep her from the valley below.

Jones was sitting near her on the rock wall. As she was leaning on her right hand, so he supported himself with his left. Their knees were facing and there was the space of a tall man's height between them.

Jones parted his long, thin lips and Mio saw his teeth for the first time. They were too large, too strong, too square and yellow for his long, pinched face. Then Mio recognized the gesture as a smile. The term, "baring his teeth," came to her. He said, "Quite a drop, isn't it?"

Mio's breath had not come back, but she would have had nothing to say if she had had the breath with which to say it.

Her silence did not disconcert him. "I'm going to throw you over, you know." His tone was conversational.

Cobham had called him a madman. Peter Davis had said it at length—unbalanced, Peter had said; a nut. But Mio had not *felt* the madness before. She caught at the air, breathed some, straightened her arm on the stone. "You tried to—harm me—on the road outside of S'Agaró, didn't you?"

"Do you expect me to admit that?" He smiled again and

this time he looked like an actor obeying the playwright's instructions: "(*Smiles, cannily*)." But he had just admitted that he was going to kill her. . . . The insanity in the abrupt reversion to a lawyer's caution was inescapable. It amounted to proof of his imbalance and in a way the knowledge gave her a kind of strength. No matter what she had thought, now she *knew*: she was dealing with a madman, and she had, if nothing more, a basis on which to deal. She said, almost evenly, "That's a very foolish way to talk, Mr. Jones. It doesn't frighten me at all, and I can't think why you should want to frighten me, anyway."

The foolish but knowing smile remained plastered on his face.

Mio wondered if her knees would hold her if she stood up, and tried to brace them. She said, "If you had any such —such foolish idea, you wouldn't warn me in advance." She made an attempt to stand, and realized that if she completed the motion she would fall. Forward?

"Don't get up—yet." He waved his hand and Mio's weight transferred itself back to her arm as if the small, arrogant gesture had been a shove. "Let me explain. There is a *point* in warning you, frightening you. I want you to make a sudden gesture of escape, you see. When you feel up to it, I want you to leap to your feet. Then I shall rush to help you—you'll obviously be excited or upset—and over you'll go."

He had very effectively removed any possibility of Mio's ever making any move at all. Not so much because she believed or feared the threat, but because his fanaticism and glacial malevolence had finally succeeded in paralyzing her.

"On the other hand," he added tonelessly, "if you *don't* make a stand, that will be even better. Then I'll come to help you up, and off you'll go. No one would sit still and let someone just push her off, would she? The very few people who will be glancing this way at that moment will see that you weren't fighting. But if you do try to fight, they'll see that you suddenly pushed me and I tried to pull you to safety. Understand?"

The light was going. Mio felt the increasing pressure of rough rock against her palm and realized that she was fainting. She brought herself forcibly back to consciousness.

"And then again"—his voice was meditative—"if you simply fall off by yourself, from fright or sheer stupidity—well, then I'll be in the best position of all, won't I?"

"Why are you . . . ? Why?"

"Oh, come now. You must have figured that out by now. Money."

"But you seem to dislike me, to *want* to harm me. To—— It seems personal."

For the first time he took his eyes off her. He looked out into the void with a look of petulant confusion and then back at her with an air of solution. "You stand personally, *very* personally, between me and the money. So of course I dislike you."

A little boy approached the edge just behind Jones, and Jones made a rapid, curious gesture; he moved not toward the child but toward Mio. The explanation of the motion came to her and a grinding sense of coldness was added to her petrifaction: If anyone interrupted him, interfered with him, Jones was going to pitch her off first and face the newcomer next.

A woman's voice called, *"Juanito! Juanito! Ven aquí! Ahora mismo!"* As the child ran to his mother, away from the perilously low wall, Mio saw the monk in the background. A fat, jolly-looking monk. She caught her breath. But—the monk was backing away. It couldn't be Cobham; Cobham wouldn't back away. *Or would he?*

It was Cobham. He took several small backward steps, and then he turned around and walked purposefully away. He walked toward an empty automobile and it looked as if he were going to get in it. The roaring in Mio's ears took the form of words: *"I am afraid of violence. Of man-made violence. . . . I don't want to kill or be killed. I want to die in bed. I want my loved ones—say, my sister—to die in bed."* His loved ones? *"For you I would strike out, or accept a blow. Or blood. Or death."*

So it *had* all been oversimplification. For Cobham, and for her. You couldn't dismiss a lifetime fear by the simple procedure of deciding that you had found a reason for dismissing it. *He* couldn't—and by his example, neither would she be able to. Not that she would have the chance.

Jones had moved into a crouch as his eyes followed the direction hers had taken. If he felt there was a danger to his plan, he would move faster, she thought. She clutched out at minutes more of life by bringing his attention back to herself. "You won't get away with it," she said as if there had been no pause. "They'll connect you with me."

"What possible connection? I'm not a lawyer. I don't represent anyone."

"I understood the connection."

"That's different. If anyone else suggested it I could laugh in his face. Much too far-fetched to stand up."

"I'd wait if I were you. This is a dangerously public spot."

"Are you humoring me? Stalling for time? Well, make the most of it. Because I'm coming over in a minute, if you refuse to oblige me by toppling by yourself. I'm tired of chasing you around. All the way from Boston. It's expensive, and I don't have your money, you know." The narrow face was insolent and petulant at the same time, but behind the petulance lay a chilling strength. The determination approaching the bigotry that had been his forefathers' showed in him as monomania.

Cobham again came into the small arc of vision that was all her frozen neck muscles permitted her. He must have been walking around, reaching for courage—and he had apparently not succeeded in gathering it. She said wildly, in the general direction of the gaunt, livid mask of frenzied purpose that she could no longer see, "How can you be like this? Why should you be like this? Why should I face someone who has become what you are? Why . . . ?" She felt the darkness and had an impulse to sink into it. But Jones made the mistake of talking. She knew it was a mistake on his part, because it caused her to listen; she instinctively listened to him instead of letting go and falling into darkness.

"You want me to psychoanalyze myself for you? You feel the need of explanatory analysis, is that it? My mother didn't love me, my father was cruel? My wife broke my heart? Well —my mother was correct and it was I who left my wife. That you do not understand me in this final moment of your existence does not seem important to me." He paused, and then with a sudden, spasmodic motion he stood up. He said, "*Now*, Mrs.——"

The blackness came; she had known it would. But it came not passively, as she had expected, but violently. It rent the air between her and the pale, convulsed man, and it brought noise with it—a rush of wind, a squealing sound, a man's shriek that rose high and faded slowly. And then she was falling. With the slowness of a nightmare she felt each small muscle and joint give; with the heightened sense that closed eyes brought her she felt the sway of her body; the wind had increased and it would be like being air-borne. . . .

Then the violence touched her, grabbed her, and it was arms. "Mio!" the arms said. "Mio!" She was being pulled savagely forward, upward.

By an intense effort of will she lifted her eyelids, looked into the familiar, dear face, and said, "Jim. You did." The face was familiar, but . . . "Didn't?" Mio asked sadly.

Westerland said, "Mio! What——" and stopped. He would be talking to himself, he saw, because the gentler darkness had finally come.

XII

"IT'S NOT A HOSPITAL," MIO SAID.

"Hello, Mio!" Mio turned her head toward the voice but realized before she found Westerland's face that Cobham would have said, "Hallo, ducks!" Westerland, however, looked warmly pleased and pleasantly pleasing. He also looked tired. His hair had managed, despite its shortness, to escape into curls, and his face seemed less strong, more vulnerable, but—strangely—older. Mio moved her head farther to the right. She was in her room in the Arycasa. There was a nun—a nurse, she supposed—at the foot of the bed.

"Not a hospital," Westerland agreed, "and that fact represents a battle valiantly won by me, with assists from Peter Davis. Finally the doctor——"

"The bearded man with the bald head?"

"That's the guy. Stubborn cuss. But he gave in. I—we thought you'd be happier here when you—you really woke up."

"How long?" Mio asked.

"The—you've been here less than twenty-four hours. It—

it was yesterday at two. It's about eleven in the morning now."

"I see. There's nothing wrong with me, is there? I wasn't hurt, was I?"

"No. Frightened, of course. Emotionally worn out. So the Beard gave you a hypo."

"Yes. I'm tired. But I could get up, I suppose?"

"Well—let's wait for the stubborn little doctor."

"Um." She pushed herself higher on the pillows and the nun came to help her. The nun had a nice face. Faces—long, livid faces . . . creased, jolly faces—floated through Mio's mind. She said evenly, "Jim got into a car, a black car, a sedan, I think—that would account for the long blackness of it—and drove Jones right off the wall." It was a statement, but it sought confirmation.

"Yes."

"And, of course, he went with him." Now the fraction of a question mark was more hope than question.

"Yes."

"Cars," she said. "I have a car-thing going. I am *used* by them—to kill and to cure."

"No, it's just——"

She interrupted: "I did Jim an injustice."

"We all did, I suppose."

"No, I mean something more immediate. He saw what was happening and he didn't come to help. I thought he was afraid. That was the injustice. I see now that he had understood, as I did, that if anyone tried to interfere Jones was going to push me off and *then* face the attack. He was—obsessed."

"Please, by what?"

"Money. If I died Arthur Jones had a chance to—to steal some money. Jim figured it out. He was right."

"I see." Westerland paused. "But really I don't see. I shouldn't bother you now, but I don't get any of it. How could Cobham know, how could you know, that Jones would push you off if someone came along? Unless Jones *told* you? And that sounds nutty."

"He was nutty, but that wasn't it. A child walked up behind Jones, and Jones couldn't know who it was. It could have been a—a challenger. Jones's first, convulsive move was toward me. He turned his head to look at whatever might be threatening his plan, but he *moved* toward me. I saw that move and understood it, and I saw Jim see and understand it. Interpret it. That was when Jim started backing away. Then he looked into a car. I hadn't any idea what he was doing, and not much opportunity to think about it. I simply decided he was deserting me——"

"That's very understandable."

"Do you think so?" Mio stared expressionlessly at Westerland. "I don't think so. I think it was unforgivable of me. Anyway, I suppose he was looking for a car with keys in it?"

"So it seems. Peter and I didn't notice him at all. We just saw you and Jones sitting on the wall, and we supposed you were talking. We had been prepared to break our necks to get back to the car if Jones showed signs of leaving without us, but as matters were turning out we simply ambled down the terrace. We never spotted Cobham at all. Not at all. I just can't understand it. He was heavy and his blond hair——"

"He was wearing a monk's cassock."

"Oh-h. That explains it. Ingenious. Well, we——"

"Why didn't you know about the cassock? Haven't they —found the—the . . ."

"Ah yes." Westerland looked at the nurse, as if for help, apparently realized she didn't even speak English, and said, "It—the car burned."

Mio's face didn't change very much, but something within her did. Westerland said hastily, "Then that black car came out of nowhere, whooshed off, taking the wall with it, and you were left with a few inches of stone in front of you. You began to sway and *then*—damn late—I started to run. I had to cover some thirty or so feet, and you very nearly were gone. It—— Well, I suppose I shouldn't talk about it now."

"It's all right. It's over. All over. Nothing to do but go on." Her voice became coldly determined. "I am going to do that with a little enthusiasm, though. No point in having a life given to you, at the expense of another's, and then not using it."

"Yes," Westerland said with the simplicity of complete confusion. Then he groped toward understanding: "He *did* give it to you, then?"

Mio looked at him with astonishment.

"We don't know anything, Mio. It *could* have been sheer accident, and simply coincidence that you three knew each other. How could we know? In a way, that confusion was helpful. It saved extra police bother. An accident doesn't get the going-over . . . When we got you down into town Ibáñez was waiting, but he couldn't be sure either, although furious speculation was making him hop like a flea."

"Coincidence." Mio caught at the word. "It wasn't coincidence that brought you there, was it? You followed me?"

Westerland didn't know why, but he wished he could say no. He couldn't. "We followed you, yes."

"Then I actually cost him his life that way too."

"Oh, now, I wouldn't think of it like that."

"I'm just accepting it. Knowing it. That's all." She paused. "I'll also remember that with almost his last words he—he committed himself to the guidance of Montserrat."

The next morning at ten, after she had given them permission by telephone, Davis and Westerland came to call. The phrase "came to call" arose in her mind because of the odd formality of their manner during the first minutes of the visit.

They found her dressed in a deep blue suit of heavy tweed, obviously a traveling suit, and surrounded by closed and stacked luggage. She said unnecessarily, "I'm off."

Westerland grinned. "Didn't think you were moving in." He too seemed conscious of the stiffness in the air and was obviously trying to dispel it. Davis leaned negligently against the doorframe, the light woodwork a becoming frame to his dark handsomeness, saying nothing, looking at Mio. Westerland added, "And what does the doctor say to your plans?"

"That I will die before the day is out. Of sheer feminine obstinacy, I gather. But I sent him and the sister off last night just the same. He was shaking his head so hard that it probably fell off in the corridor."

"No head there," Westerland assured her. "Not with a beard, anyway."

"And how are you, really?" Davis's voice was low, careless, but it held a note of concern.

"All right. Perfectly all right, thank you."

"Does Ibáñez know you're leaving?" Westerland's smile

became impish. He no longer looked so tired—she realized that he must have sat up with the nurse the preceding night —and his mischievous, youngish look had returned.

"The little señor was here at nine this morning. Frothing politely. Bobby's act in front of the Jorba has become the least of his worries. You were right about his having a listening post on my telephone, and our conversation, yours and mine, of the other morning obviously galled him. I just refused to answer all but the most obvious questions. Jim would have said that to answer questions about him, about Jim and our ride south, would have been to incriminate myself needlessly. Perfectly right, of course. So I wouldn't admit the obvious, that I had smuggled Jim Cobham up that mountain. I explained about Arthur Jones, as clearly as anyone could explain anything as confused as that. Poor man—Ibáñez, I mean." She smiled reminiscently. "He was simply an erupting fountain of questions, going back to S'Agaró and behind that all the way to the date of Jim's birth. Which I didn't know. He still would have liked to have known about Bobby, too, but Jim had equipped me for that question. As he—equipped me for so much that is—is to come. He—Jim—is being sent back to England. Ibáñez agreed to arrange it." She paused, and then the little smile came back. "There is something about Señor Ibáñez that makes me desperately feminine——"

"I think it's kindness on your part," Westerland said. "He's so small that you probably feel the need to reassure him about all Spanish males' undoubted supremacy over all females."

"A generous construction, thank you. But I have a nasty suspicion that it's nowhere nearly that nice of me. Anyway, after about thirty minutes of questioning—it's no time at all since he left here—I began to flutter. I'm not sure, but I *think* I may have shown signs of an imminent relapse."

Westerland said, "Tsk!"

"Very sensible," Davis told him.

"Yeah. Think of the poor guy. He can't prove anything, but nothing. What charge could he dream up? But providing he could—cops can always dream up something—well, she's not well; looks positively frail. And to top it off, she's American. 'The great friends of the Spanish people, the citizens of the Estados Unidos.' Currently. 'You will see how we shall make wonderful, peaceful use of these so-beautiful roads and buildings for the good of our poor people.' Yeah. And here we have one small cop daring to drag in a poor defenseless American señora, who has done nothing provably criminal, is not well, and has the outrageous nerve to be beautiful in the bargain. And not outlandishly beautiful, at that; *Spanish* beautiful, in a way all right-thinking Spaniards can appreciate. Poor little guy!"

Mio laughed with an unusual acceptance, an unusual vanity. The reconstruction was so undeniably true. "Well, I gave him a happy note to leave on. I asked him to make a record of my Paris address so that he could tell me about that—car. If it's not insured I want to pay the owners for it, of course. I suppose—even if it is insured. No reason an insurance company should be out of pocket."

Davis looked surprised. "And your fairness made him feel that you were a good and guiltless girl?"

"No, no, Peter." Westerland shook his head. "The address, so freely offered, made him feel she hadn't got entirely beyond his grasp."

"Oh." Then Davis said, "Paris?"

"Yes."

166

"You think you're well enough to drive all that distance?"

"Why, of course I——" She stopped and looked up at him.

"—alone?" Davis shook his head sadly. "Very strenuous."

Mio looked as demure as if he had been Ibáñez. "*Too* strenuous, you think?"

"Definitely. But I would be willing, at great sacrifice, to act as chauffeur."

"How kind of you. Noble. You mean you are still trying to bum that ride you asked for all the way back in S'Agaró."

"Very unkindly put. We veterans are both noble and poor and——"

"In S'Agaró?" Westerland looked at Davis. "Did he now?"

"He-did-then."

"Why the surprise, West? You didn't think I'd leave you? Well, I wouldn't have, of course."

"I'm sure you wouldn't have. No, I had another thought. Very interesting. Well——" He seemed to shelve the interesting thought. "Well," he said again, this time to Mio, "we're all packed and ready, even as you are."

"You too? You think I'd be less tired if I had *two* drivers?"

"Simple logic. Two are better than one. Also, I occasionally like Peter to know that I can get a step ahead of *him*. Just to even the scales. So this morning I got out of bed, visualized his motions of the moment, and packed my extra suit."

Peter bowed, contriving the gesture without giving up the support of the doorframe. Uncharacteristically, his light eyes held an expression, but Mio could not interpret it. Her mind was on something else, anyway; something uncomfortable. She had a feeling of foreboding, of premonition . . . She snapped the thought off as she realized that it amounted to fear. But she followed through to the point of saying to Westerland, "I shall be grateful for a chauffeur, for two chauffeurs. For your—company. Really grateful." She looked up at him and was startled by the personal quality of his small smile. Clearly he had been watching, almost following, almost interpreting her thoughts, and the smile held no mockery.

Then his mouth stretched to its usual wide grin. "So," he said, "let us now get the hell out of beautiful, sunny Spain. *Avant à Paris.*"

"A linguist," Davis said dryly, and pushed himself from the doorframe's support to reach for a bag.

XIII

THE SUN WAS HIGH WHEN THEY REACHED VICH, AND they stopped there for a late breakfast, a sort of provisional lunch. They had hoped to lunch in France, Westerland having enthusiastically nominated a restaurant in Latour-de-Carol, a restaurant he chose out of a guidebook on France he discovered in the back of the car. "A tiny town of about four hundred souls—but with a magnificent eating place. It says here. Only about five miles over the border," he added encouragingly, and tossed the book into the rear, hitting the spare gasoline tin in the process.

"Careful!" Mio said warningly. She squirmed around from her tight position in the middle of the narrow front seat so that she could inspect the loosely capped can; it had sloshed a little of its contents but had not tilted far enough to fall. "Gasoline stations will be farther apart than ever on this road. If we run out of gas, *you'll* do the walking," she threatened.

Davis spared a moment from his frowning preoccupation with the rutted road to tell her that Ibáñez would disapprove of such foresightedness. "Most unfeminine," he added, and turned his gaze back to the bigger and better holes he was trying fruitlessly to avoid. "Besides," he said, "the thing to worry about is the springs, tires, and guts of this poor piece of tin."

And then they arrived in Vich and Westerland crawled out of the right-hand side, grimacingly settled his large, jostled frame, and started off to inquire about places to eat. He grabbed a passer-by and, after five minutes of frenzied gesticulation that mildly convulsed the watching pair—neither easily convulsible—he returned to his side of the car and put his elbows on the window's edge. "The *caballero* says proudly that this town has fifteen thousand inhabitants —but they all eat at home. If we absolutely insist on being foolish, there's a joint around the corner."

The joint around the corner wasn't worthy of the term, and they faced with vast disinterest oily scrambled eggs and fatty bits of unidentifiable meat. Davis said to Westerland, as if Mio were invisible, "I see Ibáñez's point of view more and more clearly, don't you?"

"*And* the doctor's. Hopelessly, unfemininely managerial," Westerland agreed solemnly, and then turned on Mio. "Why? Please tell us *why* the Vich road? Are you aware that we'll have to climb the whole damn chain of Pyrenees before we get out of this here land?"

But, my God, Mio! That route crosses the Pyrenees!

She shook her head without being conscious of the motion. Would she always hear echoes? she wondered, and thought that she wouldn't too much mind if she did. They were almost happy echoes. She said, "I didn't want to take the Costa Brava road."

"I don't blame you for not wanting to set eyes on

170

S'Agaró, but we wouldn't have. Just before Blanes we'd have branched off onto the Gerona route. We'd be in Perpignan by now."

"But we'd have gone through Mataró, Caldetas, Arenys de Mar before we branched. I couldn't have. Not again."

"No. Well, of course." Westerland looked uncomfortable. "Sorry."

Mio didn't seem to have heard him. "Besides," she said, "I once said I'd leave by this road. It wouldn't matter, of course, and it's not like me to be—to be sentimental, but . . ." Her voice trailed off.

"Sure. Too late now, anyway. We're committed to the Pyrenees." Westerland looked down at his meat. He said wistfully, "But just think. Think of *poulet sauté Michel. Perdreau et riz.* And the *vin du pays,* in that *pays,* is Corbières. In Latour we would have had a good Collioure." His expression was that of one painfully bereft, like a child deprived of a banana split.

Davis looked at him and smiled. "How do *you* know?"

Westerland achieved superiority, simplicity, and hunger in one expressive frown. "It said so in the book," he announced with dignity.

Mio laughed with Davis. She said to Westerland, "To listen to you, one might think you had an appetite like Jim's."

"He could certainly eat, couldn't he? Well, I could *try* to match him."

She shook her head, still smiling. "Not possible."

As if emboldened by the smile Westerland said, "Mio, tell us about him. Can you?"

"Why, yes, certainly. I'd like to. All I can tell you is what he told me, of course. But that much is sad, sometimes sweet, and always interesting. Like Jim." And she repeated

171

as much as she knew of Jim Cobham. She found no difficulty in the telling, and was surprised, when she had finished, to find that her face was wet.

"So he was going to change his ways, was he?" Davis looked at a distant point beyond the small room's perimeter.

Mio brought him back. "No," she said. "He did change."

"Momentarily." The muscles of Davis's face, usually so relaxed, showed a tenseness.

"But vastly." There was infinite confidence in Mio's voice.

"Yes, that's true. So I suppose it's possible."

She looked at him quickly, but found that he was staring at Westerland. After a stretched moment Westerland looked away. Then he put down his fork and said, "Has everyone had enough of this—this—— I am at a loss for an adjective. At least, in the presence of a lady. Shall we push off?"

Beyond Vich the bad road got much worse. It also got steeper. And as they climbed it got colder. The Citroën boasted a heater, but built in with it was the European theory of what constitutes warmth. And it had no defroster, so they continually lowered windows for seconds at a time and wiped the inside of the windshield so that Westerland, who had taken the wheel, could see where he was going.

During the morning, despite Peter's and West's complaints about the route, there had been a degree of lightheartedness about the little group—partly owing to the men's desire to cheer Mio up and partly to the natural ebullience of people embarking on a trip. And it was caused partly by simple gratitude for the fact that they were getting away from what had become complicatedly unpleasant.

But now the ebullience was gone, and the gaiety. The car bounced more violently than ever because the road was hard and frozen, and the potholes lacked the muddy, squishy give of the lower country. They had climbed so high that the snow on the mountaintop was now beside them. One never thinks to attain those snows unless he is equipped with skis, rope, and alpenstock; and to reach that unwished-for, incongruous height in an automobile is disconcerting—a little ridiculous. And thoroughly uncomfortable. The sun shone brightly, imparting iridescent sparkle to the snowbanks, but it seemed to do nothing to melt or warm. The vistas were magnificent, but no one commented on them. No one commented on anything. Inside the car there was silence; outside there was silence, except for the rasping noise their passage created as the Citroën's tires ground on the frozen road.

Mio found suddenly that she was afraid.

The discovery was a shock. Twenty-four hours before she had renounced fear. She had made up her mind that she would face the world and its attacks without trembling, without craven quiverings. And now, with nothing to face, with no shock to blame it on, her interior was behaving in the old predictable way, pumping extra blood through her veins, causing her to feel violently, nervously, tremblingly alert.

She said, with a clear note of irritation—the anger that invariably overcame her at her own fears—"It's peculiarly quiet in here."

"Well"—Davis sounded apologetic—"there's so little to talk about."

She turned her anger on him. "That's a silly remark." And suddenly the anger developed a truth beyond petulance. "Silly," she said, "—farcical. What kind of dream do you fondly imagine we're in? A few days ago we sat in S'Agaró—

the *five* of us—discussing who was chasing whom. Two of those five are dead, violently dead. A fleer and a follower. And here we are, the sad little remnant of three, calmly riding along as if nothing had happened, saying that there's nothing to discuss."

Westerland said, "Mio, it's——"

"In S'Agaró," Mio said, rising coldly above interruption, "I had some sort of unformulated idea that when Jim broke us down into categories of followers and followed he was discussing good and evil. Like Dick Tracy. Cops and robbers. Murderers and murderees. But *I* was an almost-murderee, and I'm not either good *or* evil. And Jim was a species of thief, he was being followed, and he wasn't really evil. Arthur Jones embodied evil, avarice, hatred, but he was in the position of following. It . . ." Her voice stopped.

Westerland said again, "Mio." His voice was gentle, lacking its usual mischievous note. "That's all true, in a confused way, but where does it get us? Thinking about it upsets you, and what is there to be afraid of now? What——"

Mio turned violently in her seat, flinging out her hand in a gesture of protest and hitting his right arm, "*What?* Can't you see what? Who are we, the ones who are left? I had a silly feeling of balance—if one of you two was evil, then the other must be good. So childish of me. If one of you is the Astra thief—and murderer—then the other could be a—a hijacker, or whatever they call them. Not justice triumphant, but evil riding with me."

In the cold silence that followed she saw her foolishness clearly. What safety could she have hoped to evoke by bringing it out into the open? She might have ridden serenely into Paris and picked up life as she planned to pick it up. But therein lay the answer; she could not postpone living. If she were going to start living, she must start now. And, foolhardy or not, she was no longer afraid.

Westerland said, "I see your point." His voice was still gentle, but there was an odd note in it. He sounded—Mio fumbled toward understanding—almost hurt. He took his eyes briefly from the road and for a fraction of a minute their long green regard rested on her face. She felt inexplicably warmed and reassured. He said simply, "I really don't think you have anything to worry about."

"There!" Davis said. "You have The Word. And if it doesn't put you entirely at ease, let me add my peseta's worth. I personally wouldn't hurt the tiniest fraction of a hair of your black head." He, too, was looking down at her, but Mio didn't meet his eyes. "In fact, I might step so far out of character as to court trouble in an effort to protect you. My-lady-fair business."

"Well." It was ridiculous to be embarrassed. The sensation reminded her of the time she had questioned the intelligence of driving Jim back to Barcelona. She had been right to question then; she was right now. But . . . "My apologies to both of you. And don't belittle yourself, Peter. You indisputably fought in the war, didn't you?"

"Well, I was pushed. It was easier to go forward than to back up."

"You know," Westerland said, "I'll bet there was an element of that sort in the Astra affair that Mio seems unable to put out of her mind."

"I don't get the connection." Davis sounded lazy.

"Maybe he found it easier to go forward than to back out."

"Um. But murder is damned far forward, don't you think?

175

You still cling to the genius theory, don't you, West? And you still want to discuss it."

"I find it challenging. The ingenuity. I was only trying, in S'Agaró, to get you to admit that an ingenuity existed so I could show you up before Mio with the greater brilliance of my theories."

"I'll bet," Davis said obscurely. Then he added, "So you figured out the three-hairs business, huh?"

Westerland looked briefly away from the road to glance at Davis. "Well, no. But neither did you."

"Thought about it afterward."

"Did, huh?"

"Uh-huh. The armored car stopped, didn't it? Must have since there was no sign of a crash. Unorthodox, isn't it? I believe those drivers' first oath is that they will stop for nothing but traffic lights. Nothing. Not even for a cop unless he's standing at an intersection directing traffic. And cops know about that rule, understand it, and don't flag down armored cars. So I wonder what could have halted them? A barrier? They would either have crashed through a barrier, or showed signs of hitting it. The car was unscratched, wasn't it?"

"So?"

"Well, if I wanted to stop such a car I would have considered the basic nature of man, and taken it into account. And then I would have bought a large blond doll, crumpled it a bit, put a little catsup on it, and laid it in the middle of that empty road, where headlights would fall on it."

Mio's head swung toward Westerland. He said slowly, "Would you, now? That would have been very clever of you. Yes, very intelligent figuring." He paused. "Now I'll show off. The way the Astra men died. The authorities must have known the cause of death. There was a theft, so death was caused by a human agency; deaths caused by man are detectable by autopsy; *ergo*—the method of death must have been known."

"And, *ergo* and all, just where does that get you?"

"It simplifies the next step. What manner of death would have left corpses that puzzled inexperienced viewers —that is, unprofessionals, non-medical men like cops and reporters?"

"Your previous suggestion was poison," Davis said dryly.

"It was a negative suggestion. But how about electrocution?"

The silence came again. Mio looked at a snowbank and thought that it was the first time she had seen snow in Spain. Was it the lack of air in the car or was the tenseness causing her shortage of breath?

Davis offered her a cigarette and lit it for her. His manner was abstracted. When he spoke it was as if there had been no pause. "Electrocution seems pretty smart."

"As a solution? Or as a device?"

"Both—or either. Let's see—that Pittsburgh road was the route to the Gillingham plant, wasn't it? In fact, a large percentage of the money was Gillingham pay roll. The rest was other pay rolls."

"Yes. And where does that lead you?"

"To the power lines along the road."

"Hm. A man sitting atop a power line, all equipped— insulated electrician's gloves and so forth—attaches a considerable length of the correct weight of wire to the power line. Another man grabs the end—perhaps it has a rope attached to it—and waits *across* the road. At the proper moment, after the doll has performed its function, he lets go.

. . . Two points: how could they be sure the car would be grounded, and how come they could leave no traces? Witnesses didn't see traces."

"You can't answer those points, West?"

"Daring me? Well, the guy on the pole could have stayed up there until the job was done, wound up the wire, and come down in time to leave with the others."

"Sounds possible. Long way down one of those towering poles, so that would have been his only function."

"Um. And as for grounding the car . . ." Westerland frowned.

"For the split second that everyone in the car was concentrating on the doll, someone could come from the rear with a device. Some sort of device? I'm no electrician."

"Neither am I."

This silence threatened to be permanent. Mio already felt like Pandora. Recklessly she pulled the lid wider open. "And the cleaned road? You said it had simply nothing on it. That it had been swept in some way."

"Vacuumed," the two men said together. Then they laughed together.

Mio's head went left and right as if she were watching a miniature Ping-pong game. "Smart, aren't you?" she commented toward the neutral ground of the windshield.

"Yes," Davis told her, and said to Westerland, who hadn't opened his mouth, "Stop bragging and do something useful."

"I'm driving and deducing. What more do you want?"

"Puff harder on your cigarette."

"What for?"

"Warm things up." Davis looked down at Mio. "If," he said, "a guy was electrician enough to figure out the elec-

178

trocution bit, he could probably manage to fit his car with a makeshift vacuum cleaner. Width of the car or wider, maybe. See?"

"No," Mio said.

"And," Westerland said slowly, "an electrician, our Madigan."

There was another brief silence. Then Peter said, "Really . . . ? The name is spelled with one *d*, by the way. Unusual spelling."

"I know."

Mio looked up at the face of Peter Davis and thought it was almost beautiful. But there was something missing from it. "Is your name Madigan?" she asked.

The light, expressionless eyes looked down into hers. "I said I was no electrician, remember? I am Peter Alan Davis, duly so christened. In fact, for a little group of—peculiar people, we bear a minimum of fake names. When Jones was introduced I had a moment's hope that we were getting into the realm of Pseudonymania——"

"That," Westerland interrupted, "is the kingdom bordering Walachia?"

"—but," Davis said, "he really was a Jones, it seems. We're all honest, you see——" He stopped abruptly, and a silence grew.

Mio said, "You know. You both know. That I'm wearing a fake name."

"Ibáñez told us," Westerland said. "He was angry, you see." There was a faint note of apology for Ibáñez in his voice, and no other discernible emotion. "Does it matter?" he asked.

"No. It doesn't matter at all."

"I was sure it wouldn't." His sideways glance was a composite of many things. Like Cobham's expressionful glances. One of the ingredients of this one, she realized, was pride. And found the realization pleasant.

. . . But if Peter wasn't Madigan . . . She kept her head turned to the left and looked up at Westerland's profile. It was ruggedly irregular, with none of Peter's classical symmetry. Nor was there any of Jim's blandness in its strength. In response to her steady regard he grinned down at her. There was a defiant Cobham-like gaiety in the grin, and she felt hopelessly confused. "Look," he said. "That view!"

He brought the car to a standstill and they found themselves on a level stretch, the first level spot in many miles. To their right was a densely wooded area, but on their left was a great valley—or a series of valleys, as descending slopes met others and dimpled together to form further descents. The car seemed, in fact, to be on top, on the uppermost of all the crescendoing "tops" that they had labored to climb and that were now spread gently and innocently beneath them, looking deceptively mild—mere rolling swells. Westerland said, "It's . . ." and gave up the hope of finding words. In an attempt to express scope he swept an arm in as wide a gesture as the small car and their cramped positions permitted.

Mio recoiled—from the gesture, from the view. Views, she thought numbly, were not a thing she would appreciate for some time. She ricocheted heavily off Davis's arm and said, "Sorry," as he said, "Whoops!" He juggled his cigarette, came in contact with the lit end, said, "Ouch!" and bounced the cigarette violently upward. There was a little flashing reflection in the windshield, and a sizzling noise. Mio felt heat on the back of her head and instinctively leaned forward and put her hand on the nape of her head. There was a roar, and with the roar came the shock.

Mio went upward. Her head hit the hard-top roof and as she came down she saw the shattered windshield beneath her—she was going to fall on the jagged edges. But she didn't. Westerland got there first, twisting his body in front of hers and absorbing the shock. There was blood on his face. The first roaring sound had diminished but it had not ceased. Over it Westerland shouted, "You take her, Peter! Your side, safer!"

Davis took her, by the hair and shoulder, and she was dragged out onto the roadside like a sack. As they gained the little hump of the roadside's edge, he stumbled and fell heavily, and she remembered that he had only one leg. He got up quickly, however, and pulled her to her feet. He said, "All right?" and then dragged her backward again. Westerland came then and climbed the mound on her other side. He also said, "All right?" and gave her a chance to nod. She was, she realized, entirely all right. Except for a headache. She probably had a lump on the back of her head as a result of having hit the roof.

They stood, their backs to the dense trees, and watched the car blaze.

Davis said, "Will the forest catch, do you think?"

"Think not." Westerland was mopping at his bloody face. "Far enough, even from that intensity. Are your cuts bad, Peter?"

"Cuts?" Davis sounded dazed. Mio looked up at him and discovered, at the same moment he did, that he was slashed around the throat and ears. "No," he said. "At least they don't hurt." He pulled out a handkerchief and dabbed at his neck.

"The gasoline," Mio said. "In the can. In the back. It wouldn't close properly. The can. It sloshed. Remember, Chris? Remember how it splashed? When you——"

"Yes, my dear. But it's all right. *We're* all right."

"I had a premonition," Mio said. "I knew. I was relieved when you two said you'd ride with me. Cars. They burn. They hit walls. They go over walls. I knew. I could have told you. That's why I was glad of the company—because I knew. But I didn't want to be afraid of things. So I didn't admit it. Didn't admit that we lose cars the way we lose people." She laughed. The tinkling laugh echoed off the trees and sounded ridiculous. The words sounded ridiculous, but she was unable to stop talking. "I mean, we lost two people and now we've killed two cars. Or they kill us. Or try to. My parents. Even Charlie. Although that wasn't a car. But Jim was in a car. Now this one's failed, but one will try again. This one's gone, but——"

"*It's gone! It's going!*" Davis sounded even more peculiar than she did, and she shut her mouth and turned to look at him.

He had taken a step forward and his profile, lighted by the flames, had a strange look of urgency. She had never seen Peter look urgent, she realized. *That* was what was missing from his face. Life.

On her other side Westerland stepped forward until he was parallel with Davis. He put an arm in front of Mio and touched Davis's arm. Davis turned to look at him, the painful urgency still etched into his face. Westerland said, "Forget it, Peter. It's gone. Where was it?"

"Under the floor boards in the back."

"Well, then, it was the first thing consumed. Forget it. You know, until Mio told me you had tried to hitch a ride

north with her, I thought it was—there." He pointed downward. Mio followed the directional line of his finger and
watched as Davis tapped his right leg. There was a very faint
tinny sound.

"Here?" Davis asked. "How old-fashioned of you, West.
I thought you were so clever you'd discard that silly idea—
and so that's exactly where it was. Until I became afraid of
a personal search, and a beautiful stranger showed up—so
beautiful that no Spanish customs guard would . . ." His
voice trailed away and his eyes went back to the inferno
that separated them from the incongruously peaceful countryside. He stared blindly.

Westerland said, more forcefully, "Forget it, Peter."

"*Forget* it?" Davis took another step forward. "But that's
just what I wasn't going to do any more. It—— I was going
to use it to—to purpose. Purposefully. I . . ." He stared at
the holocaust, and didn't step back as the remains of the
car's roof sagged drunkenly toward him.

Westerland said, "Wrong purpose. That wouldn't gain
you—what you want."

"But I've got to try, to make the effort." He took one
more step forward, which brought him to road level and almost within reach of the intense flames.

Mio came to life. She reached down and yanked his arm.
Physically the tug barely moved him, but it did seem to
catch at his attention. He turned and looked at her. Their
eyes were on a level. "It wouldn't help, you think?" He
wasn't talking to her.

Westerland said, "No. Hinder. I would have taken it away
from you anyway, you know. Was it all there?"

"It might have hindered me," Davis said, his eyes on

Mio's. Who was the hypnotist, who the hypnotized? she wondered. "Yes. But the effort, the push . . . ?"

"No!" Westerland said forcefully. "How much was there, Peter?"

"He gave about a fifth of it to the others. There were four others. And spent some. Not much. Wasn't easy, as Cobham said. Had to be dumped on foreign black markets, since he knew that anyone legal would have the numbers of pay-roll bills. There? Almost a million, I guess."

"Did you find out for yourself? Or did he tell you?"

"Who?" Davis finally looked away from Mio, transferred his staring gaze to Westerland. "Oh," he said, "Madigan." He took a deep breath, climbed back up on the mound beside Mio, and looked down into the flames. "I found out enough to be suspicious, although I didn't know what of. Then, when he was dying, he told me. Incidentally, he gave it to me, willed it to me. Although I realize the impossibility, the insanity of that, from your point of view." Into the silence that followed he dropped a few more words: "From any point of view."

Westerland didn't answer.

The car burned as if it would never stop, although there seemed little left to burn. Through the red and yellow flames they could see the steel skeleton, at times glinting bluely. Mio thought regretfully of her clothes, and then was grateful for the normality of that reaction. Or was it normal? Should she be thinking of the million dollars that was apparently burning under her nose? She couldn't, because she couldn't encompass it as a fact. She could think only that the three of them hadn't been hurt, although the cuts on Peter's neck had looked quite nasty, worse than the scratches on West's face. She turned to her left and for a second thought Peter wasn't there. She swung farther around and found that he had stepped farther back, so that he was now on the very edge of the wood behind them. She said, "Peter."

Westerland's voice came over her shoulder. "You're leaving?" he asked. He sounded—— Mio groped for the explanation and then had it: West sounded sad.

"Not much point staying, is there?" Peter's voice was wistful, as if he wished West would show him a point, give him a reason for lingering. He retreated another few steps, so that there were a few trees between him and them. "Will you follow me, West?" he asked, and the wistfulness was still there. It was, Mio thought, almost an invitation.

"Peter!" she called. "The cold! And your neck! Peter . . . !"

But he was gone.

Mio swung violently back to Westerland and caught at his arm. "West!" she cried. "Go get him!"

Westerland didn't move. He examined her face and then said remotely, "For justice's sake?"

"Justice? No, no! For *his* sake. It's cold. He's bleeding. He has only one leg. He'll die!"

"No." Westerland looked down at his arm, and Mio realized she was tugging at his sleeve. She dropped her hand. "He won't die," Westerland said. "I'd waste a lot of energy, and what for?" He looked intently down at her. "What for, Mio?"

"He meant well! He *means* well." She groped for a persuasive argument. "When Jones came to Barcelona after me, and up Montserrat after me, *he* was the first to follow. You just followed him. If it hadn't been for Peter, I'd have been alone. With Jones. *That's* a reason, isn't it?"

"I would like to agree. I do agree that if he had thought

of it he might have followed to keep you safe. *If* he had thought of it. But he's not a man who thinks. And—you know, don't you?—he was following the money, not you. He had put it there." He nodded at the remnants of the still-burning car. "Under the floor boards." He smiled abruptly, an odd, almost tender smile. "Under the floor boards," he repeated. "Only Peter Davis could have done anything so haphazard. So lazy. So—trust-to-the-breeze."

"But you *like* him. You're fond of him. You understand him. You can't just let him—walk into nowhere like that."

"I'm fond of him." He looked away from Mio, over her head and into the forest. "We understood each other, he and I. We were even alike. Except for one thing: He was the hunted, I, the hunter. 'Some people are born to be hunters; there are others whose destiny is decided before their stars have merged, and it is preordained that they shall flee.' Who said that?"

"West! For God's sake, don't quote things! Go after him! He's your *friend*."

"My quarry." His voice was cold. "But for once," Westerland said to the woods behind her, "I'm going to forget that. He'll move along easily, slowly. He won't waste effort, or expend unnecessary energy. And he'll find someone who'll take care of him. Or someone will find him. The drifters always get taken care of." He paused, and then his attention came back to the moment and he looked down into Mio's small white face. "If I tried to follow," he explained more gently, "I would blunder violently along, because I'd have a goal—as he doesn't. And if I found him, I'd have to arrest him. Arrange for extradition. Would you like that?"

"Arrest him?" she whispered. "You're—the Government? The United States Government?"

He smiled suddenly, a gay, flashing, warm smile. "Well," he said, "not quite. But a fraction thereof. And here—on this little bit of road—perhaps I *am* the symbol of it."

"Then"—she clung stubbornly to the thought that Westerland's strength could accomplish anything and that Peter should not be left alone in the forest—"isn't it your *duty* to go after him? To catch him?"

"I don't think so. Duty is interpretable. I have—lost Peter. The real Peter, the one I almost caught with my mind. And I have certainly lost the physical Peter, and anyway what purpose would his arrest have served? The money is gone." He nodded again at the smoldering car. "He didn't steal it in the first place. He should have turned it in, of course. But such an uncharacteristic going-out-of-his-way was more than could be expected of his particular species of human nature." He stepped off the mound, looked unseeingly at the ruined car, and then turned to Mio and held out his hand. "Come on, Mio."

She stood stubbornly on the ridge, as if she planned to take root there. "Come on where?"

He looked at her silently, intently, and then he smiled— a quick, elfin grin. "I could say, 'To the border.' It's only about five miles, I figure. But suppose I borrow some of your drama and say, 'To life'? What was it you said? 'I am going to live with enthusiasm. No point having a life given to me at the expense of someone else's, and then not living it.'" He kept his hand extended toward her.

Mio looked absorbedly into his face. Abruptly she took a deep, gulping breath, as a child does after it has stopped crying. Then she smiled slightly, but, slight or not, the smile did more than usual to warm her face. She put her hand into his and stepped off the mound.

187

As they started up the road, he tucked the hand under his arm. "The exercise should keep us from freezing," he said. "Is that suit warm?"

"Yes. What about Peter? Will it be colder in the forest?"

"I really don't know. I'm a city man. Maybe the trees will cut the wind, or maybe they will deprive him of the heat of the sun. I simply don't know. But I do know he'll be all right. . . . Those are nice sensible shoes. Did you plan a hike?"

She wouldn't be diverted. "He'll be all right physically. I'm beginning to believe you on that point. But what about his plan for living? He was going to have a—a goal."

"Don't you know what the goal was?"

Goal? It came to her that she did know, and she looked up at him with shock.

He nodded. "You. I didn't approve of that. And if he had failed to attain it, he'd have been right back where he was before."

"I see." Mio put it away to think about later. "And you," she asked. "Does this—this failure matter very much? To your—your work?"

"Failure? It's not quite that. I saw the money burn—I've no doubt of that. So maybe the insurance companies can reach a compromise. And now that we're sure it was Madigan—we weren't before—we can probably start from that knowledge and round up Madigan's associates. May get the other quarter million back in large part. No—not quite a failure."

"I see." Mio looked across him and so across the mountainside. The atmosphere was limpidly clear and the view was beautiful. She could discard the fear of views, too, it seemed. And of cars. She *had* had the premonition. But such superstitions were wrong and—— She smiled: right or wrong, that superstition was gone. Cars no longer seemed threateningly poised to destroy her and those she loved. The fires, the walls, the precipices, the fears, were behind her.

So far the exercise was keeping her warm, and she marched sturdily along the road. But she was grateful for the support of Westerland's arm. She thought of the arm, of herself, and of their utter isolation.

"We're so alone," she said vaguely. "We were five in S'Agaró, and now we're only two."

"Two." He nodded. "Two is a good number."